BUILDING A CONSCIENCE

BUILDING A CONSCIENCE

LAWRENCE KEOUGH

Copyright © 2024 by Lawrence Keough.

All rights reserved. No part of this book may be reproduced, stored, or transmitted by any means—whether auditory, graphic, mechanical, or electronic—without written permission of both publisher and author, except in the case of brief excerpts used in critical articles and reviews. Unauthorized reproduction of any part of this work is illegal and is punishable by law.

ISBN: 979-8-89031-252-5 (sc)
ISBN: 979-8-89031-253-2 (hc)
ISBN: 979-8-89031-254-9 (e)

Because of the dynamic nature of the Internet, any web addresses or links contained in this book may have changed since publication and may no longer be valid. The views expressed in this work are solely those of the author and do not necessarily reflect the views of the publisher, and the publisher hereby disclaims any responsibility for them.

One Galleria Blvd., Suite 1900, Metairie, LA 70001
1-888-421-2397

To my wife, Jackie; children, Joel, Ryan, Kyle, Sara, and Mary; parents, Lawrence and Carole; brothers, Michael and Timothy; teachers; coaches; colleagues; and close friends who have encouraged me to think beyond myself for the common good.

CONTENTS

Ch. 1	Brokering the Deal	1
Ch. 2	Understanding Bethany	11
Ch. 3	Luke's Ascension	16
Ch. 4	Battling for the Court of Public Opinion	27
Ch. 5	Corey Unwittingly Plants Seeds for Luke	43
Ch. 6	So Much for Best Laid Plans	48
Ch. 7	Meredith Crazy like a Fox	57
Ch. 8	At Crossroads	61
Ch. 9	A New Direction	69
Ch. 10	Preparing for the Inevitable Confrontation	73
Ch. 11	Luke's Strategy	77
Ch. 12	Luke's Next Step	89
Ch. 13	Trouble on the Home Front	92
Ch. 14	Luke the Environmentalist	105
Ch. 15	For Better or Worse	118
Ch. 16	A New Beginning	134
Ch. 17	Sunset Cruise	149

CHAPTER
1

BROKERING THE DEAL

As Luke McAlarney approached his retro-looking, twelve-cylinder Jaguar sports car, he clenched his fists with a fervor rush and demonstrably raised both arms much like an athlete celebrating victory. He turned over the engine and momentarily listened to the throaty sound emanating from the dual exhausts as he tapped the gas pedal. He shifted the 5.3 litre engine into gear as he exited from the Palm Beach constituents' office of U.S. senator Mack Belue, chairman of the powerful Senate Ways and Means Committee.

Senator Belue had delivered the news Luke had been anticipating for weeks. There were sufficient votes for SR 538—"Creating Jobs and Lowering Fuel Costs"—to move through the Senate Ways and Means Committee for favorable passage in the full Senate following Congress's summer break in six weeks.

The omnibus legislation with landmark implications would lay the legal groundwork for the installation of a two-thousand-mile pipeline stretching from Canada into the American heartland of twelve Midwestern and Southwestern states.

Luke was on a natural high as a surge of adrenaline pumped through his body while he processed the news and what it meant for him, personally and professionally. Luke felt a profound sense of gratification. Certainly, a promotion and substantial pay raise would be forthcoming.

His mind was racing with excitement as he told himself as the senior lobbyist for Petroleum Energizing North America, he would be in line for the coveted executive directorship of PENA's governmental affairs operation, an array of legislative advocacy resources ranging from old-school mobilization efforts to all facets of communication within social media.

It would be a coup, Luke mused. But while accelerating onto I-95 toward his palatial home in the posh Bel Aire community in Palm Beach, his Kodak smile was supplanted with a scowl as he sardonically acknowledged that highfalutin titles are bullshit. His mind tracked to the sobering reality that the only real thank-you in this godforsaken business was the paycheck directly deposited in his bank account on the first and third Fridays of every month.

Luke, who looked his age, 44, with a middle-aged paunch and a receding hairline that foretold male-pattern baldness, was indefatigable in his work ethic while embracing Charles Darwin's theory—survival of the fittest.

Luke was highly motivated to succeed because no accomplishment came easy for him. He was afraid to fail, and fear was a great motivator for him to succeed.

As a middle-school student, he was not precocious in the classroom, on the athletic field, in band, or on the theatrical stage. Try as he did, Luke could not find his niche.

His inability to flourish made him an insecure, shy, and unconfident middle-school student.

And if that were not enough to dampen his spirits, Luke received the sobering news as a then fourteen-year-old student in eighth grade that he had been cut from the Lake Worth Middle School basketball team.

Luke was emotionally crushed with the realization he was unworthy to be a member of his school's basketball team and, as such, extricated from his friends who made the team.

Luke felt utterly defeated, which led to a heart-to-heart conversation with his father, Dermot.

Dermot consoled his son with sage advice: "It is better to have tried and failed than to have never tried."

Dermot promised his son if he outworked his competition, he would eventually ascend from mediocrity.

Dermot, an attorney who had worked his way through law school, explained there is a fine line separating the rank and file from the very best in virtually every field.

Luke remembered his father telling him ascension occurs when people reach within the depths of their heart, soul, and every fiber to give of themselves beyond the expected norm.

Luke heeded his father's advice. The fierce desire Luke demonstrated on the athletic field as a high school athlete was parlayed in a different arena where the score was calculated by the number of legislative bills he successfully lobbied on behalf of PENA.

In retrospect, Luke was convinced his extrication from the basketball team was a blessing in disguise. Absent that setback, the father-son talk that placed Luke on an upward trajectory likely would not have occurred.

Luke realized at a young age that from the agony of defeat were lessons for a lifetime that bode for a silver lining.

Luke knew his silver lining would be realized if his internal fire were to continue to fuel his tireless work ethic. He realized the movers and shakers were not the most gifted and eclectically talented people in society, but those who had above intellect and driven with unbridled ambition.

That is why he was the ubiquitous lobbyist, awaiting an opportunity to meet legislators in a coffee shop, at a local watering hole, in the hallways of the congressional office building, at political gatherings, or even on a golf course.

Luke was a survivor in the cutthroat world of big-money and high-powered politics. His profession, if he could call it that, demanded waking up at dawn to communicate to a network of supporters and sucking up to power brokers with ingratiatingly polite posts on Facebook, Instagram, Twitter, and via e-mail. His daily conquests were euphemisms for apologies, mea culpas, brownnosing, and mind-numbing humility in a cesspool known as his work environment.

Luke was known in political circles as an effective and accomplished lobbyist. However, much of the lobbying accolades bestowed on him coincided with the U.S. Supreme Court's precedent-setting case legalizing unlimited amounts of money channeled from anonymous donors to political action committees to political candidates.

The ruling in the Citizens United case provided a quid pro quo—special interest groups deliver big bucks to candidates and incumbents; elected officials respond with obligatory political favors and unfettered access.

Luke was the point person in such interworkings for PENA. It was his job to ensure congressional members honored their end of the bargain.

PENA and other powerful special interest groups established super political action committees, which were no longer regulated under the terms of campaign finance laws. There was a mad dash for special interests, through super PACs, to receive unlimited sums of money from individual citizens, corporations, and unions to influence voters by spending exorbitantly on negative political ads and, in doing so, determine the outcome of political races, thereby effectuating public policy and federal spending.

PENA had carte blanche to direct money to its super PAC. The exorbitant contributions were held in abeyance for the expressed purpose to line the pockets of select members of Congress.

Luke ensured PENA's super PAC contributions were placed in the right hands, and congressional members were aware in no uncertain terms that PENA was the cash cow. Once that groundwork was etched in stone, Luke followed up, hell-bent for PENA to get its monetary return by having clandestine language buried in one-thousand-page bills and effectuating votes in Congress.

On the heels of Citizens United, Luke expended little time on grassroots mobilization efforts to influence congressional members. America as a representative democracy made good fodder for political speeches but did not constitute the framework for a high-powered lobbyist to deliver salutary results.

Luke knew within his professional world, America had become an oligarchy in which a top-to-bottom mode of politicos, money brokers, and special interest groups influenced public opinion that determined the outcomes of political races, resulting in their desired policy and/or budgetary outcomes.

Regardless of Citizens United and the ungodly amount of money that determined political races and public policy decisions, Luke was in a bottom-line business, and he once again delivered with SR 538 positioned to move through the labyrinth of the U.S. Senate.

Luke pondered an impending pay raise and how it would allow Bethany, his wife of twenty-two years, to continue jet-setting to Cancun and hobnobbing at the Bahia Mar Country Club in Palm Beach. And Luke reminded himself the extra money would ease the financial burden of $40,000 in annual private school tuition at the prestigious Montgomery Preparatory School for the couple's two teenage children.

As Luke approached the gated Bel Aire community he called home, he attempted to communicate with Bethany on the Bluetooth in the Jaguar. When she did not answer, he left a message, with a hint of excitement in his voice, asking her to go to the wine cellar to open their coveted 1928 French Chateau Saint-Pierre to celebrate a monumental occasion.

Luke expected Bethany to greet him with a glass of wine in hand as he walked into the vast and ornate foyer ensconced with white marble floors and a gold-plated chandelier. He could hear her voice echoing from the high-arched ceiling as he began ascending the spiraling staircase.

"Bree, I am not going to discuss this with you now. Talk to your father when he comes home."

Bree, formally named Brianna, was the sixteen-year-old daughter of Luke and Bethany.

Bree saw her father at the bottom of the staircase and traipsed down to greet him.

She leaned toward her dad and said in a hushed voice, "Mom is impossible. She does not get it that I really need to go to Jamaica with my friends."

Bree had been pampered within a microcosm of privilege and affluence throughout her young life.

And like many teenagers, she had an inflated view of herself as if she had the hutzpah and worldliness of a cosmopolitan woman.

And try as Bethany did to convince Bree otherwise, the daughter responded with supercilious omnipotence, turning a blind eye and deaf ear to her mother's premonitions about a world rife with iniquity.

Luke winced in response to Bree's attempt for him to side with her. Bree not only was Daddy's little girl, but she also had him wrapped around her little finger, or so she thought, to get what she wanted.

"I don't know about this, Bree," Luke said. "Can we discuss this later? I need to talk to your mother now."

Bree, who looked like a younger version of her mother with auburn-colored hair and baby blue eyes, knew delaying the conversation outside of her mom's earshot was in her best interest.

"OK, Dad, whatever," Bree said while giving her dad a peck on the cheek and adding, "Glad you are home."

Luke smiled at Bree and then looked upward at Bethany, still standing at the top of the staircase. She looked pouty as she gazed at her husband's playful expression, flipped her hair like a runway model, and demurred, "I could use some good news, Luke."

"Well, my dear, I am indeed the conveyor of good news," Luke gleefully and playfully responded. "We have the votes for the cross-continental pipeline to become law. It is not a done deal, but we are damn close to the finish line."

Bethany, who maintained a curvaceous figure, looked like she belied her actual age of forty-three.

She then asked if the good news translates to moving forward with purchases that have been put on hold due to a dearth of available cash.

Luke responded by sarcastically elucidating Bethany's excessive lifestyle, "You mean your liposuction procedure and your regular trips to Manhattan to shop at Armani's and catch a random Broadway play."

Bethany hesitated as she pondered whether to refute Luke's sarcasm then responded, "Very funny, Luke, but you promised me a new car, one that accommodates the kids and me. The Audi is just too small."

Luke interjected, a bit of irritation in his voice, "You know, Bethany, the sedan is only a year old, and we owe more on it than its value. What do you have exactly in mind?"

She slowly approached him, accentuating her sinewy figure and then placing her mouth against his right ear, whispering, "Range Rover."

Gold digger came readily to Luke's mind as he told himself that he married a woman who would never be able to satisfy her insatiable appetite for material wealth.

CHAPTER
2

UNDERSTANDING BETHANY

A s Bethany made her demands, Luke recalled her impoverished roots.

Bethany was raised in a poor working family in Moultrie, a small rural town in Southwest Georgia known for its antique shops and historic sites. As a teenager, Bethany had one pair of jeans, a skirt, a Sunday dress, and a combination of T-shirts and blouses she mixed and matched.

Bethany's austere upbringing was the impetus for her fixation for opulence.

She knew she had to marry into money and set out to obtain her "MRS" degree at Emory University, a private college in Atlanta that attracted students from affluent southern families.

Bethany was a good student and received an academic scholarship in nursing, which paid for her tuition. She qualified for a student loan that was utilized for housing and textbooks. To cover ancillary expenses and a modest allotment in spending money, she earned a couple of dollars an hour plus tips as a waitress in the student union cafeteria.

Her parents, Wyatt and Savannah, had to scrape and claw, living paycheck to paycheck, to make ends meet. They did not have the financial wherewithal to subsidize their daughter's college education.

Wyatt sold used furniture, and Savannah cleaned homes for upper-income families.

But come hell or high water, Wyatt and Savannah made a long-distance phone call to Bethany every Sunday evening. And they ensured their daughter received a handwritten note and a crisp $20 bill for her birthday each of the five years she was an undergraduate at Emory.

Bethany always was appreciative, not for the dollar amount per se, but for the loving gesture from her parents to part with money they could scarcely do without.

Bethany, upon arriving at Emory, knew one of her first orders of business was to pledge a sorority associated with an upper-crust fraternity.

By her sophomore year, Bethany was a little sister at Chi Omega. The charter of Chi Omega stipulated social events with Delta Pikes. It was inevitable that Bethany and Luke, a brother of Delta Pikes, would cross paths. When they did, Bethany portrayed a contemporary version of Scarlett O'Hara as a beautiful, seductive, and mercurial southern belle.

Luke was in no position to resist. The couple became engaged within a year and married once he was offered a Grooming Young Entrepreneurs business grant from PENA. In those early years, the newlyweds were able to live off proceeds from the grant and financial support from Luke's parents, Dermot and Mary.

Luke, whose keen instincts served him well as a lobbyist, should not have been surprised that Bethany's impoverished youth would make her yearn for material wealth.

In retrospect, Luke should have expected Bethany's reaction when he expounded upon the news of the pipeline and his impending bonus and promotion.

Luke turned his attention from bygone times to the present in which he could feel the caress of Bethany's hands around his neck and her heavy breathing as she placed her lips close to his.

But Luke was not buying Bethany's seductive kit, at least not on this evening.

"You know, Bethany, I want to give you what I can, but an $80,000 SUV is not in our budget," Luke said.

Bethany's mood quickly turned irascible as she placed her hands on her hips, bluntly telling Luke to purchase the vehicle for her.

"I deserve it," she demanded, sounding like a spoiled adolescent. "I am sick and tired trying to keep up with other wives, who have no problem getting what they want from their husbands."

So much for an evening of celebration. In what began as stupendous news had quickly devolved as the McAlarneys were well on their way to trading salvos in a protracted acrimonious exchange.

Suffice to say, Luke was in no mood to hold back. "You did not marry one of those other guys who has a blank check for anything and everything that his wife wants. You married me for better or worse."

Luke then cringed, immediately knowing that reminding Bethany of her wedding vows was like pouring gas on an open fire.

"Luke," she asserted, "you knew when we married I did not want to live a life of austerity."

It was more important for Luke to retaliate with a verbal jab than to diffuse the argument. "The girl I married was a registered nurse who contributed to our household income, but she quit the nursing profession to be a full-time housewife, freely spending money I earn."

Luke knew his comment was well over the top.

At that point, Bethany turned on her heels and walked into the bedroom. Luke, taking a deep breath, headed to the refrigerator, clutched a cold beer, opened it, and moved to the family room where he sat in a La-Z-Boy. In a seemingly reflex action, he grabbed the TV remote on the arm of the recliner and clicked to Ship Shape, a program for boating enthusiasts. He had a great affinity for boating because it allowed him to escape from the world in which he lived.

Following Ship Shape, Luke perused pictures, saved on his iPad, capturing a scuba diving trip to the Florida Keys and a big game-fishing expedition in the Bahamas. He nostalgically studied the pictures of himself and noticed a genuine smile and happiness. As he leaned back in the La-Z-Boy, he commiserated—"those were the days, those were the days"—before falling asleep.

CHAPTER

3

LUKE'S ASCENSION

The following Monday, Luke caught a red-eye flight from Palm Beach International Airport to LaGuardia, where a limousine was parked outside the baggage claim for him.

The driver signaled to Luke, who walked a beeline to the open door of the limousine.

"Good morning, Mr. McAlarney. Nice to see you back in New York," said Alfred, who had been driving Luke to and from LaGuardia for years.

Luke asked, "Alfred, can you get me to the corporate office within thirty minutes?" Alfred smiled then said, "You know I will or die trying."

The limousine arrived at PENA's corporate office with five minutes to spare. Luke grabbed his briefcase, which contained an iPad with sufficient gigabytes of memory to store a proposed twelve-state agreement for the installation of the pipeline.

As Luke approached PENA's front-door entrance, he heard the words "excuse me, excuse me, mister." Luke turned to see a man standing at the street curb.

"Can you spare a cup of coffee and something to eat?" said the destitute-looking man, whose face was badly chapped, presumably from sun exposure. His clothes were wrinkled and emanated a stench that suggested they had not been washed for days.

Luke reached in his wallet and handed the man a $5 bill.

"This is a start," the man pointedly and seemingly ungratefully retorted.

Luke visibly shook his head in disapproval of the man's comment while entering PENA's building. Luke was pleased with himself. He kept a few dollars in his pocket for such occasions. In his mind, this was preferable to contributing to need-based organizations, particularly in light of the substantial limitations on charitable contributions in the tax code.

Moments later, Luke approached Lindsay Garmin, executive assistant for PENA's chief officer, Chester Ferguson. Lindsay was a reticent, middle-aged woman whose long brown hair was pinned in a bun as if she were emulating the plain-Jane look.

But Lindsay was naturally attractive with oval brown eyes, a pug nose, and slender figure. However, unlike other women in PENA's central office, Lindsay did not ensconce herself in expensive jewelry and high-end clothing. Her outfits were plain and ordinary compared to the Versace, Vuitton, and Louboutin lines donned by her coworkers.

Lindsay's wardrobe may have been out of financial necessity than personal choice. There were whispers her husband was an unemployed alcoholic.

Lindsay's drab clothing could have been an issue for an executive assistant employed in an upscale corporate office in the hub of Manhattan if it were not for her high competency and professionalism. She was a wiz with Excel spreadsheets, organizational flowcharts, personnel records and as Chester's scheduler.

Lindsay greeted Luke with a warm smile and extended her right hand as a cue for him. He did not flinch, taking her hand to his lips for a playful kiss, which had become their signature greeting.

For Luke, the greeting was all in fun, but for Lindsay, the flirtatious play was a nice respite from her strained marriage.

Lindsay and Luke made small talk, and then she pointed to the double doors that were the vanguard for Chester's office.

"Mr. Ferguson has stepped out of his office on three occasions, asking if you had arrived," Lindsay softly said. "You need to see him," she added as her eyes fixated on the double doors.

"OK, OK, I can take a hint," Luke relented.

As Luke opened the double doors, he gazed at Chester, seated behind a mahogany-laden desk. The veneer reminded Luke of his father's Chris-Craft speedboat, a real head turner built of Philippine mahogany wood.

Chester, a slender man with brown thinning hair and a mustache peppered in gray, looked more like a college professor than a CEO, especially when he discarded his suit coat for a buttoned plaid sweater, which he sported on this particular day.

Chester walked around his desk, and he and Luke exchanged a robust handshake. Chester placed his left hand on Luke's shoulder as he effusively praised him for his lobbying prowess.

Chester added that PENA's board of directors was anxious to hear from Luke today via Skype.

Luke thanked Chester for his kind words and explained, "Well, controversy over the Affordable Care Act, as well as disclosures related to the Patriot Act, provided us with much-needed cover."

Luke, choosing his words carefully, said a slow-recovering economy also helped PENA's cause.

"Linking the installation of the pipeline with reducing the unemployment rate, creating more jobs, and potentially flat-lining the price of fuel at the pump were all win-win," Luke said. "I assured everyone on Capitol Hill that the pipeline would create twenty thousand immediate jobs and the opportunity to exponentially add more jobs during the installation of the pipeline and afterwards."

Luke had distributed a blueprint indicating the number of jobs that would be created by laying the pipeline through and/or around 212 cities or townships. Unskilled and semiskilled labor would be needed in each of the cities as PENA coordinated the project with its engineers.

Beyond the initial laying of the pipeline, PENA would construct refineries and maintenance oversight, leading to additional jobs in a second phase.

Congressmen representing each of the districts in which the pipeline would be installed were promised a specific number of jobs for their constituents.

"It really came down to political expediency in which we made an offer congressional members could not refuse," Luke told Chester. "This is a classic example of a short-term solution both politically and economically."

Chester began fumbling through his desk looking for his coveted pipe and tobacco. Chester saw the pipe next to a cleanly wrapped Cuban stogie. He held the stogie as if it were a trophy and gestured for Luke to partake.

Luke had vowed to kick his tobacco habit to the proverbial curb. But he knew his best interactions with foes and friends were done when they discussed business over a cigar in buildings that permitted smoking.

Luke could not intelligibly explain why mutual smoking built camaraderie, but he knew there was some inexplicable and intangible that made it happen. His inability to define how smoking ameliorates relationships reminded him of U.S. Supreme Court Justice Potter Stewarts's comment in which he famously said he is unable to define pornography, but "I know it when I see it."

Luke knew timing was everything in life, and his commitment to kick the habit would have to wait for another day.

"Why not," Luke said with a smirk, responding to Chester's offer for him to indulge.

He puffed on his cigar as Chester lit it. Chester allowed Luke to take a few more puffs then asked, "Can we assume OWL will reinforce our media campaign with news coverage about the installation of the pipeline?"

OWL, one of the big three twenty-four-hour news networks, was reputed for backing corporate America and parroting the drumbeat that environmental regulations were job killers and the death knell for big business.

"Don't worry about them," Luke responded. "They are salivating at the bit to push the pipeline to fruition and, in doing so, stick it to the president."

"Good to hear," Chester emphatically retorted.

Luke elaborated as he disclosed OWL was willing to review PENA's video feeds to determine if some or all of them can be parlayed into news coverage of the pipeline.

But Luke added OWL also was preparing to launch its own series of hard-hitting pieces.

"Just the same, Luke, you offer them anything they need to do a full court press as our media campaign is unveiled," Chester said.

"You know I will, sir," Luke said.

If the issue of pipeline implementation were a sporting event, PENA had hit the ground running in the first half of competition. However, the outcome was still in the throes of uncertainty as the second half was yet to begin.

But Chester and Luke feared if PENA's media campaign stalled, then passage of SR 538 in the

Senate would not be pro forma. It was essential for the legislation to receive favorable passage in both houses of Congress because the president refused to sign a permit through an executive order for the pipeline to be implemented.

The media campaign also was critical to build public pressure on the president such that he would not veto SR 538 if and when it reached his desk.

To suggest PENA had a lot riding on the media campaign was an understatement.

Chester sighed and then looked at Luke. "We are obviously pleased with your work to successfully position the legislation for favorable passage. You wisely directed our PAC money to key Democrats and provided them other perks that led them to abandon their political relationships with the environmental groups opposing the pipeline."

Chester was particularly impressed with Luke's stratagem for high-quality video feeds to be released to local news programs across the heartland in which select Democrats were depicted as job creators.

Chester, looking pensively with his head cocked slightly to the right and his eyebrows raised, asked about political pressure that might be brought to bear by environmental rights groups clamoring about fracking, impact on wildlife, farmland, and potable water.

Luke responded they do not have a bully pulpit at the moment with the big media focused on health care and national security–related issues.

"But could they?" Chester anxiously asked. Luke acknowledged that they could emerge at some point and become a problem.

Chester then patted Luke on his back and said, "It is your responsibility to ensure they don't become a problem."

Chester then added, "Luke, the board today is prepared to offer you a promotion with a considerable pay raise. But you must know this is contingent upon you fulfilling all phases of the process until the project reaches fruition."

Luke was not surprised. He knew ultimately the board's evaluation of him would be based on the full body of his work. He also was well aware he would be evaluated on what he can and can't control, regardless whether that is fair.

After each board member was Skyped into the conference call, they were congratulatory, and their facial expressions reminded Luke of the idiom in which the cat swallowed the canary.

Luke thanked each board member for the kudos then cut to the chase by asking if he would have the full arsenal of PENA's public relations resources to inundate the public with messaging as if it were the gospel truth.

"We are going to dress this up like a pig with lipstick," growled board member and Texas oil tycoon William Joseph Payne, known as Billy Joe. "When you get through with all your fancy PR spin, Joe Lunchbucket will see the pipeline as American as apple pie."

Luke, mulling over Billy Joe's comment, knew the PR campaign would have to hit hard with the pipeline as a job creator.

"We know," Luke said, clearing his throat, "one in four construction workers were unemployed in the twelve states that the pipeline will be implemented.

"We know the total number of jobs that would be created, but I am not sure how that specifically translates to out-of-work construction workers to be employed through pipeline infrastructure."

The congratulatory plaudits and good will that kicked off the conference call seemed like ancient history. Board members were chiming in with directives for Luke to get up to speed with the PR campaign as soon as possible. This was most evident when Marvin Rothenstein, a New York lawyer from the prestigious law firm of Cohen, Sullivan and Rothenstein, representing big oil and big banking, opined, "Luke, you would be well advised to become more conversant with all of the job-related data as soon as possible."

"It will take me a few days to get up to speed after receiving the news in the past forty-eight hours that Congress will favorably pass the legislation," Luke responded.

Luke regretted the comment as soon as he spewed it, knowing he would be perceived as defensive and thin-skinned.

Chester quickly stepped in, adding, "What Mr. McAlarney means is he will be right on it."

Chester asked board members when they wanted to follow up with a conference call. They unanimously agreed to convene in a week to stay abreast of Luke's progress with the PR campaign.

Luke was not surprised but was feeling the heat. He had just come off an eighteen-month pressure-packed series of intense negotiations with Congress and the administration.

After the videoconference concluded, Luke told himself, "I always will be on the hot seat with this group. But then again, that's why I am paid the big bucks."

That thought sparked a wry grin.

CHAPTER

4

BATTLING FOR THE COURT OF PUBLIC OPINION

Three environmental groups—Green Spaces, Protecting Mother Earth, and Our Nature-Our Future—had released media statements they were mobilizing thousands of constituents in select towns where the thirty-six-inch-wide pipeline would funnel 830,000 barrels of crude per day from Canadian oil sands to U.S. Gulf Coast refineries.

Luke, through PENA's public relations department, countered the media releases with strategically placed op-ed pieces in state dailies and blogs that were covering the impending installation of the pipeline.

Luke and PENA's communication director, Meredith Delaney, hammered home the point that job growth is an economic necessity. Their message was cloaked in sentiment that those who oppose the pipeline were not friends of working families and, as such, were out of touch with real-life Americans in the heartland.

Moreover, PENA's message was to depict environmentalists as more interested in hugging trees than providing jobs for families in need.

This inference was a brilliant stratagem because it preyed on the fears of those who were counting on the pipeline to infuse dollars into their households. Luke and Meredith, a thirty-something woman who knew what to say and when to say it, was a master at delivering communiqués that created sharp lines between apparent good and evil.

Her plan set into motion accusations from families in the Midwest. Many of these families took Meredith's inferences to the next level, just as she hoped they would do.

A young mother in Steele City, Nebraska, one of the cities projected for job growth based on pipeline implementation, expressed sentiments of blue collar families when she questioned whether anti-pipeline protestors were real Americans.

"The protesters are not the friends of law-abiding American families who simply want an opportunity to be gainfully employed to support themselves," said Peggy

Norton, the wife of an unemployed construction worker and mother of two preschool children.

Mrs. Norton, quoted on the front page of the Register, Steele City's daily newspaper, excoriated the protesters as un-American who have a leftish environmentalist agenda that places the welfare of wildlife over human beings.

Mrs. Norton graced the front page of the Register as she held her three-year-old son in one arm and pushed her baby daughter in a stroller. In the photograph, she appeared harried with her long brown hair tousled and her face betraying her youthful facial features.

As Meredith examined the photograph, she contacted Luke on speed dial.

Luke picked up the call on the first ring and said, "What is it?"

"Luke, you need to look at the Sunday morning Register," implored Meredith. "I believe we have found our poster girl for our job growth campaign."

"I am looking at the story on my iPad," Luke calmly and stoically responded while eating breakfast with Bethany and the kids. "Our girl appears to be a little rough around the edges."

"Exactly," retorted Meredith. "She is perfect. We need someone to carry the message that is one of them, not someone who is refined in the social graces of aristocracy."

"I suppose you are right," Luke added. "You are the expert in such manners. I will defer to you."

Luke's remarks brought a faint smile to Meredith's face.

"You won't regret this," Meredith told Luke.

Luke reminded Meredith they are joined at the hip in the PR campaign. As the phone call ended, Luke noted the irony that his professional relationship with Meredith was much like his rapport with Chester.

Everything hinges on the bottom line, Luke thought.

He chucked to himself, remembering the famed quote—"Just win, baby"—from the late Al Davis, who was majority owner and GM of the Oakland Raiders.

If the PR campaign were to be auspiciously jump-started, it would be the result of spin control in Steele City. PENA had set up mobile units to interview for crew positions, and environmental groups had signaled that Steele City would be one of their initial rallying points.

Luke and Meredith agreed to meet in Steele City on the following Monday.

They reviewed talking points, indicating the obvious: the pipeline would stimulate the U.S. economy and enhance energy security, emphasizing a new pipeline is the cheapest, safest way to transport dirty tar sands from Canada's booming oil fields to U.S. refineries.

In order to hit a home run, Luke and Meredith would have to define the pipeline on their terms. Meredith verbally walked Luke through other notable PR campaigns to underscore the importance of defining the language.

Meredith said that as the Bush administration was preparing for military action in Iraq, military support was equated with national security and weapons of mass destruction. And she added, as if she were standing atop her soapbox, the messaging was cloaked in an orgasmic cry of patriotism, and anyone who was opposed to the war was labeled with the broad brush of unpatriotic, un-American, and a sympathizer of the tyrannical and evil dictator, Saddam Hussein.

"Let's examine the messaging in the prochoice campaign," Meredith said. "The messaging is not about abortion but about a woman's right to choose."

"Terms such as unborn child or baby that induce an image of an infant," Meredith said, "are supplanted by medical nomenclature that does not invoke passion, emotion, and feelings of the taking of a human life. That is why terms and phrases such as fetus and termination of pregnancy have become the rite of passage for the prochoice movement."

"I get it," Luke retorted, with a hint of vexation in his voice as if he did not need to be instructed in Meredith's didactical version of PR 101.

"If history has taught us anything," Meredith noted, "whoever prevails in the court of public opinion wins the war."

"That is why it is imperative we deflect environmental messaging by defining the pipeline on our terms as an economic recovery package that addresses the nation's energy needs for decades," she said.

Luke and Meredith knew their ace card was a sluggish economy.

But their support, at best was based on political expedience. If environmentalists were to hijack PENA's job growth campaign, the PR battle could be redirected into a grassroots effort to amend or table SR 538.

It was not as if the pending legislation was impervious from derailment. An effective outcry from concerned citizens, coordinated by environmental groups, could lead to a successful attempt to eviscerate funding for the pipeline.

Luke knew he had to look no further than the Affordable Care Act to realize that a bill favorably passed by Congress, signed into law by the president, and affirmed by the U.S. Supreme Court can still come under intense scrutiny that threatens its implementation.

Luke looked at Meredith and said there are unknowns that will ultimately turn the tide of public opinion.

"The first," Luke said, "is whether our messaging will be effective. The second unknown is the effectiveness of environmental campaigns, backed by scientific research asserting that the pipeline would endanger water supplies by contaminating aquifers."

Luke knew environmental scientists were preparing to render a compelling argument why the pipeline would exacerbate climate change by contributing to global warming through the emissions of carbon and other greenhouse gases into the atmosphere. The argument was backed by the perceived aftermath of strip mining of forests in which tons of earth would be extracted, contaminating barrels of freshwater and burning large amounts of natural gas.

Luke and Meredith turned their attention to promulgating their message via Twitter, blogs, AM radio, and most importantly, with OWL News. Meredith provided Luke with a montage of PENA's videos that would be presented to OWL and other broadcast and journalistic enterprises.

As Meredith hit the Play button to view the first video, she winked at Luke and said, "Our goal is to blur the lines between PR and news such that our vignettes are perceived as actual news conducted by OWL."

After watching a series of vignettes, Luke was pleased and affirmed Meredith for a job well done.

"This is packaged quite well," Luke said. "They certainly can be perceived as OWL news feeds. I really like the way the vignettes appear to be objective news reporting."

Meredith reminded Luke that in the spin game of public relations, the message has to be believed by the rank and file, not necessarily factual.

"At the end of the PR battle," Meredith explained, the environmentalist camp may very well have the scientific facts to back up their claims.

"Our message resonates because people want to believe that the pipeline is the answer to their financial woes," Meredith said. "When it comes down to brass tacks, people are going to be more concerned about their immediate needs than future ramifications on the environment," she said.

Meredith added that old-school media as the watchdog -- to do investigative reporting with the breadth and depth of Bernstein and Woodward in Watergate -- was practically nonexistent.

"In modern media, it is about pitting people against one another. Liberals vs. conservatives, rich vs. poor, blacks vs. whites, women vs. men."

Meredith knew contemporary cable news was an avant-garde to meld journalistic enterprise with theatrical entertainment. Each of the big three cable news networks was under the auspices of entertainment-news conglomerates.

Meredith had no doubt the power brokers on the entertainment side demanded the infusion of shock, drama, and partisanship into cable news programs to drive ratings and procure profits.

There was a paradoxical twist Meredith acknowledged was borderline genius: Although viewers received packaged news that is more form than substance, they tuned in for the partisan agenda, incivility, and overall entertainment.

Meredith was struck with the irony: win-win for the conglomerates' board of directors and stockholders, lose-lose for the viewers as they were deprived of the breadth and depth of real news.

In her heart of hearts, Meredith was saddened that the mixed marriage of entertainment and news had devolved into a reality television saga.

She was convinced that intertwinement of entertainment and news spawned HBO's Newsroom. Meredith said the media of yesteryear had a liberal bias as it attempted to report a sharp contrast between good and evil and right from wrong.

"But contemporary news," she said, "is about false equivalency in which both sides are pitted against one another even though one side's position may be factually baseless."

She cited global warming. One side offers scientific facts: Global temperature is rising; glaciers are melting; seawater is rising; more and more carbon is released in the atmosphere; the ozone is deteriorating.

Luke, intently listening to Meredith's unofficial media seminar, interjected, "What are you saying, Meredith? We are on the wrong side of the issue because science does not support our message?"

Meredith grinned and said, "Like you, Luke, I am on the side that pays."

They both laughed, then Meredith added, "My point is the false equivalency works to our advantage."

"Thank God, we don't have to deal with investigative reporting that could expose our message," she said.

Luke asked Meredith to predict the outcome of the PR battle.

Meredith hesitated then said, "We should be OK if we stay the course. But it only takes one misstep or, God forbid, a scandal to change everything."

In the immediate weeks ahead, the battle lines were drawn sharply as both sides descended in Steele City in an effort to get a leg up in the court of public opinion.

The confrontation would pit families promoting jobs against families supporting the environment. Inevitably, mothers such as Peggy Norton, with their young children in hand, would be face-to-face with their environmental counterparts.

Mrs. Norton and her delegation arrived in Steele City on the Friday before Memorial Day weekend. There was a hustle and bustle in the air as thousands descended into the city. The city's best were out in full force, directing an overflow of vehicular and pedestrian traffic. Every hotel in the downtown district displayed No Vacancy signs.

Many of the automobiles were decorated in placards. One vehicle, an older model station wagon, had a spray-painted message on both sides: "Save the Indigenous Black Bear." The station wagon was owned by Claire Adams, a fifty-something woman with long brown hair strewn in gray, tied in a ponytail. Her significant other, Ansel Blahut, was behind the wheel as the vehicle slowly passed Peggy Norton and her contingency.

"Look at those tree-hugging hippies," Peggy shouted. "They love trees more than people."

Ansel turned to Clare and asked, "Are we going to take that?" Claire, without hesitation, retorted, "We are going to teach that bitch a lesson in civility."

With that, Ansel shoved the gearshift into park, engaged the handbrake, and exited the vehicle. Ansel, who was wearing a flannel shirt, approached Peggy and then stopped within an arm's length of her. He then unbuttoned his shirt and exposed his bare chest. Adorning his chest was a tattoo in the likeness of a wolf.

Peggy was ambivalent while gawking at Ansel's chest. On one hand, she thought of Ansel's chest as a canvas of artistry. A smile appeared on her face as she asked herself if the circus were in town.

As Ansel stood unemotional and detached, Claire approached Peggy with a packet of literature and stated, "Good afternoon. I hope you will receive this information for which it is intended."

Claire then extended her arms, attempting to offer the information to Peggy much like a track athlete extending a baton to a teammate in a relay.

But Peggy refused to accept the information as she placed her hands on her hips in speechless indignation.

"As far as I am concerned, you can take your animal-loving propaganda and put it where the sun don't shine," Mrs. Norton said. At that moment, Peggy's son, Travis, put his hands over his ears and yelped, "Mom said a bad word."

"Lady," Claire said, "you are setting a very poor example for your children. Please reconsider and read the information. You just may be enlightened."

Peggy then reached into a duffle bag strapped onto her shoulders and said, "What is good for the goose is good for the gander. Take our information and read it."

Claire accepted the information with grace, attempting to alleviate any antipathy between her and Peggy.

But neither woman offered a handshake as a farewell gesture before they parted company.

As Claire walked to the station wagon, she turned to Ansel and said, "Game on."

The next day, one of PENA's videographers, Ralph, a stocky man in his late forties, was shooting video of Peggy for news feed.

Meredith had provided Peggy with a potpourri of sound bites for her to spew to media. Peggy, with her children at her side, looked a bit jaded as she stood on the steps of the Steele City Court House amid hundreds gathered for the rally.

Peggy glanced across the street and saw Meredith and Ralph. Meredith gave a thumbs-up signal, and Peggy followed her script. Ralph hustled across the street to shoot several minutes of close frames featuring Peggy.

Ralph shot additional footage of the crowd, targeting those with placards supporting the installation of the pipeline. It was only 8:45 a.m., and Ralph was heading to the nearby PENA van where he downloaded the video and posted it on YouTube. He also inserted the video on several blogs that were ghostwritten by Meredith.

Meredith also sent the video of Peggy as a news feed to broadcast media in the states where the pipeline would be laid.

In the next twenty-four hours, Meredith included sound bites from business leaders and local politicians who touted the pipeline as essential for those in the heartland.

The video was aired by OWL on several news shows within a twenty-four-hour cycle. Meredith, following Twitter and various blogs, said an estimated 20 to 23 percent of the respondents interpreted the video not only as actual news but also as no spin.

"It does not take much for a percentage of the viewers to buy into our agenda," Meredith told Luke in a text message. "These viewers are already with us and just need the video to support their preconceived opinions."

Meredith's video also was forwarded to local broadcast stations, especially those that don't have the financial wherewithal to cover news stories and events.

Nearly all these stations inculcated the video within their news segments within the same day.

After the long day, Luke and Meredith met at Mae's Coffee Shop on Main Street in Steele City to debrief. "We pulled it off," Meredith said, brimming with a smile that would make proud any toothpaste manufacturer.

Luke, pulling on his right earlobe, was less enthusiastic. His assessment: PENA has a leg up in the public relations campaign.

"But we have a long way to go," he deadpanned. "We'll have to check the proverbial scoreboard after going through this in dozens of cities within the next ninety days."

Luke's words were prophetic.

Luke may have received a premonition when Bobby Reynolds, a Democratic congressman from Chicago, contacted him a few days earlier. Congressman Reynolds, like other members of Congress, had been assured PENA would deliver jobs to his constituents for pipeline installation.

But Congressman Reynolds wanted more, much more. He asked Luke for an unspecified contribution. Known as a duplicitous politician with reputed ties to the underworld, Congressman Reynolds was too cagey to attempt to extort money, but he intimated there would be a price to pay if Luke and PENA did not financially deliver.

His comments had an eerie feel to them and made Luke feel uneasy.

But Luke did not want to establish a specious precedent in which politicians dictated the terms in which PENA would pay them.

Luke contacted Chester to find out if there were internal leaks from PENA that Representative Reynolds may have received.

Chester's immediate response was no. But he told Luke he would conduct an inquiry with each member to ensure PENA's inner sanctum was airtight.

Chester did his due diligence, speaking to each member and circling back to Luke.

"Just what we expected," Chester said. "No leaks on our end."

Luke and Chester agreed to undertake a hard-line position with Congressman Reynolds, calling his bluff and, moreover, sending a message in no uncertain terms that PENA does not offer contributions in response to veiled threats.

CHAPTER
5

COREY UNWITTINGLY PLANTS SEEDS FOR LUKE

Luke and Meredith parted company for a few days of respite. Luke boarded a 6:00 p.m. flight to return home. He arrived at Palm Beach International Airport a few minutes before midnight. In short order, he located his car, placed his luggage in the trunk, and sat his weary body in the driver's seat. As he steered the Jaguar out of the parking lot, he wanted to hear a discordant genre of cacophonic and bombastic rock 'n' roll that would shoot a rush of adrenaline in his lethargic state of mind and body.

But instead of listening to the iconic music of his youth, his Sirius radio was tuned to a Christian radio station.

"Who the hell has been playing with my radio?" Luke asked himself.

Then his mind flashed back to giving his eighteen-year-old son, Corey, the keys to the Jaguar to drive to a friend's home. Luke recalled Corey indicating he and a friend were listening to a Christian radio program about the Ten Commandments as an assignment for their Sunday religion class.

Luke recollected that Corey appeared interested in organized religion. And Luke affirmed Corey for that interest.

In this day and age in which a teenage son can potentially become involved in drugs, alcohol, sex, pornography, and guns, Luke was pleased he was not having a conversation with his son about the aforementioned.

But Luke wanted to know the impetus behind Corey's newfound interest in religion.

The next morning, Luke asked Corey to join him for breakfast. After a little cajoling from Luke, Corey reluctantly agreed to converse with his father while sipping on orange juice and eating toast.

Luke asked a couple of sundry questions about Corey's summer vacation heretofore and whether he was hanging out with his friends from Montgomery. Then Luke changed the subject and began the first of several questions intended to elicit Corey's motivation to learn more about religion.

"Dad, our religious education teacher has asked us to listen to Christian radio," Corey said, turning his head to look squarely at his father. "This is more of a request than assigned homework."

Corey expounded, hoping an explanation would lead to his father to cease and desist.

"I have been studying with some of my friends. One of our interests is religion," Corey said.

When asked to identify the friends in the study group, Corey acted sheepish, his face turning a bright crimson.

"Actually, Dad, the study group is me and Shannon," Corey said. "She is a friend, and we have a good time studying together."

I bet they do, Luke thought, amused by Corey's reluctant candor.

Luke decided to have a little fun with Corey, asking if he and Shannon were kissing friends.

The question made Corey squirm as he defensively replied, "We are just friends."

Luke knew that further questioning at Corey's expense would be cruel and unusual punishment for any teenager.

Then Luke placed his hand on Corey's shoulder and said, "Your mother and I love you and are very proud of you."

Luke could not deny Corey's comments had struck a chord with him.

Although Luke was raised Roman Catholic and Bethany as Southern Baptist and they were married in the Catholic Church, their passion was a deity of a different sort. They had left their spirituality at the altar and had no intention of looking back.

On the surface, Luke and Bethany had been climbing the social ladder to join the ranks of the nouveau riche. They were obsessed with living the American dream of power, privilege, and wealth.

If the McAlarneys' home nestled in an upper-crust community were an indication, the dream appeared to be coming true. Their four-thousand-square-foot home was replete with an indoor bar, Jacuzzi, game room, and mother-in-law suite. The exterior featured a screened-in swimming pool and tennis court juxtaposed to the PGA golf course.

Their neighbors were a venerable virtuosic list of who's who among movie stars, celebrities, professional athletes, and movers and shakers of Fortune 500 companies.

They were running in the same circles as the socialites of Palm Beach via the Bahia Mar Country Club, exclusive parties, art festivals, musicals, and charity events.

But Luke and Bethany were more concerned with perpetuating an image of wealth than actually being rich. Regardless of their net worth, Bethany was obsessive about playing the role of matriarch in a very public way. That is why she was so fastidious to post pictures and comments on Facebook, Instagram, and Snapchat of their home, yacht, automobiles, and their vacation hot spots in Las Vegas, New York City, Virgin Islands, Cancun, and the Bahamas.

In the confines of her home, Bethany was fond of saying that image was not the only thing, it was everything.

But in reality, the McAlarneys' income did not match their opulent lifestyle. They were drowning in debt. And like most couples under financial duress, Luke and Bethany had heated arguments over their financial matters.

But Luke's conversation with Corey was a reminder that money is not the be-all and end-all. He thought about that conversation and realized there are some things in life money can't buy.

Luke smiled and told himself, "Corey bared his soul about his crush on Shannon and their mutual interests in religion. That is priceless."

CHAPTER
6

SO MUCH FOR BEST LAID PLANS

Although Luke's discussion with Corey was refreshingly memorable, he was preparing to do what was needed to win the battle for the pipeline to be a done deal. His first order of business was to inquire how Meredith was faring as the public relations battleground had moved from Steele City to the Patoka and Wood River areas in Illinois.

As Luke speed-dialed Meredith while sipping on his morning coffee, he expected to be reassured the momentum and support from Steele City was carrying over in Illinois. But Meredith's words were the antithesis of confidence and reassurance.

The initial words from Meredith were "Luke, I can't talk now. I am in crisis mode as the PR campaign is careening out of control. Our support has eroded, and we have been rocked back on our heels by a team of scientists who have effectively debunked our message." She said this hurriedly as if she were in a panic.

Luke interjected, "What the hell are you talking about, Meredith?" Luke could hardly believe he was talking with the same woman who just days ago was confidently discussing PR strategies as if she were a Nobel laureate in communicative messaging.

Now Meredith was seemingly in an act of desperation.

"I am preparing to do whatever it takes. You can count on me," she said with audible emotion.

"Meredith," Luke countered, "listen to me. Pull yourself together, and don't do anything until I arrive in Patoka. Is that clear?"

But Meredith refused to heed Luke's directive.

"Desperate times demand desperate measures, Luke. I have to go," Meredith said as she ended the call.

Luke immediately scheduled a flight reservation, but the earliest he could arrive in Patoka was late evening.

As if the conversation with Meredith was not enough bad news, Luke received a phone call from Meredith's videographer, Ralph, just prior to boarding his flight.

"Mr. McAlarney," Ralph said, "I am sorry to bother you, but you need to know what is happening here."

Luke braced for foreboding news.

"Meredith has hired fake reporters who report bogus information and then pitch it to OWL," Ralph explained. "It is only a matter of time before OWL realizes our video feeds are a total fabrication. And Mr. McAlarney, as you know, when OWL discovers this, our relationship with them will be forever severed."

As Ralph attempted to expound on the aforementioned, Luke cut him off.

"Ralph, I usually do not take kindly to people calling out their fellow employees," Luke said. "But under the circumstances, thank you for sharing this information with me. I need to board a plane now."

The videos Meredith shared with Luke were rife with PR spin but were grounded in elements of the truth.

Luke wondered if Meredith had unveiled a set of totally bogus videos.

What Ralph did not disclose to Luke was his leak to one of Congressman Reynolds's emissaries, Jerry Butler. Ralph and Jerry had been friends since grade school and drinking buddies for decades.

Ralph did not have much of a filter as most of his thoughts were impulsively spewed to his longtime friend without contemplating the consequences of sharing sensitive information that an opportunistic shark such as Congressman Reynolds would exploit for pecuniary gain.

Although Jerry swore on his mother's grave that Ralph's secret was safe with him, Jerry predictably spilled his guts by cathartically sharing with Congressman Reynolds the sordidness of the fabricated news feeds.

Jerry did so in hope he would be rewarded as a loyal sycophant.

Rebuffed by Luke, Congressman Reynolds directed Jerry to shake down Meredith in Patoka.

Jerry, a scrawny man with a truculent demeanor, stalked Meredith on State Street in Patoka.

"Hey, lady, slow down," Jerry said, trying to catch up with Meredith as she briskly walked toward the concierge in the lobby of the hotel where she was a registered guest.

Jerry was miffed with Meredith for her ill-fated attempt to flee from him. As he caught her, he grabbed her shoulders, shook her, and yelled, "Relax, I just want to talk with you!"

Meredith was petrified as she looked at the concierge and beseeched him to call 911.

Jerry then whispered in a voice only Meredith could hear, "You better tell your friend to put the phone down, or I will blow the whistle on your fake news operation." Meredith blurted to the concierge, "It is OK. Please put the phone down. This was all a misunderstanding."

The concierge, a young man only two weeks on the job, gave Meredith a blank stare, then reluctantly ended the call.

Jerry then escorted Meredith to a nearby exit. The conversation was short and to the point. He told her to make four cash deposits in a specified bank account.

Meredith was to deposit $5,000 within forty-eight hours and $15,000 each of the next three weeks. She realized her career would go up in smoke unless she contained the scandal. And she knew Luke would go to Chester if he were informed.

Meredith decided to attempt to meet Jerry's demands. She made the initial payment then tried to buy time to come up with the second payment.

She called Jerry, offering to pay him in services other than a cash deposit. He knew better than to accept Meredith's offer.

"Maybe a different time, place, and circumstance," Jerry told himself. He directed Meredith to pay or suffer the consequences.

Jerry waited an additional day. But when Meredith did not deliver the cash, he contacted Congressman Reynolds, who exhorted Jerry to continue to pressure Meredith to pay up.

Congressman Reynolds had no intention of containing the scandal. He marshaled his cadre of sources to strategically leak news of the scandal. In the political inner belt of D.C., the news spread like gas dosed on a runaway fire.

Meanwhile, Luke had boarded the flight to Patoka and sent a text to Meredith, indicating they would meet at the Palace Bar, a watering hole adjacent to the hotel where Meredith was staying.

When Luke arrived at the Palace minutes before midnight, he surveyed the bar and saw Meredith seated on a barstool in a low-cut black dress with a cigarette in hand and a drink within ready reach.

As he approached Meredith, she turned and asked, "Where the hell have you been?"

Before he could respond, Meredith went on the offensive.

"Why can't men show a modicum of respect for career women?" she asked with indignation in her voice. "It is past midnight, and I have been waiting for you in this godforsaken place for hours."

"OK" was all Luke said, unsure of Meredith's state of mind and not wanting to exacerbate her fury.

Luke, attempting to be more of a big brother than a boss, tried to comfort her, reaching for her hand and asking the bartender for a cold water bottle. Meredith ingested most of the water and then leaned into Luke, whispering, "Would you be so kind to walk me to my room? I have a splitting headache."

Luke clenched her right hand and helped her from her seat.

"Let's get you to your room for a good-night's sleep," he said in his best nurturing, caring voice.

As they entered Meredith's room, she excused herself, heading to the bathroom.

Meredith was visibly inebriated. Luke assumed she had too much to drink and would sleep it off.

But Luke was not prepared for Meredith's next move. She appeared from the bathroom, less her dress and panties. Meredith, completely nude, provocatively positioned herself on a nearby couch.

She suggestively asked, "What is the matter, Luke? Does the cat have your tongue?"

Luke was aghast at Meredith's audaciousness. He was uncomfortable with her nakedness but could not help admire her well-shaped form.

Luke considered Meredith an attractive woman as she dressed to the nines to accentuate her figure. But as she stood in all her glory, he swallowed hard as he was in an ambivalent state. He tried not to ogle at her, but his eyes were transfixed on her nudity. He did not know if he was more captivated by her natural beauty or audacity.

But Luke was not about to be bamboozled into a tawdry escapade. His mind began to race with a plethora of questions and thoughts. What would Bethany think if she were to find out? How do I let Meredith down without impacting her fragile psyche?

The questions forced Luke to transition from a myopic to lucid state. He knew he had to rebuff Meredith's sexual advances by making an exit.

But before Luke could do so, Meredith made a catlike move in one seamless motion and locked her hands around his neck.

"I am not going to let you go," she said with a devilish grin as she kept one hand around his neck and grabbed the crotched area of his pants.

But Luke was not grinning. He was grimacing in pain from the stronghold she had on him.

Luke gave Meredith a hearty push, and she abruptly fell on the floor. Her head flew back, and for an instant, Luke thought she was injured.

She appeared unscathed from any physical injury. But as she sat on the floor in her birthday suit, she screeched in her highest-pitched shrill, "Get out, get out of here, you SOB."

It was apparent her nude folly had left her with a bruised ego.

On cue, Luke quickly turned on his feet, opened the door of the hotel room, and did not look back. He knew his departure was morally responsible, both professionally and personally.

But as he headed to his rental car, he shook his head in disbelief while contemplating Meredith's meltdown.

"How could she become a basket case so suddenly?" Luke asked himself.

CHAPTER

7

MEREDITH CRAZY LIKE A FOX

Luke knew Meredith's unraveling was symptomatic of a larger problem in which the campaign was in great peril, and as such, the pipeline and his future were imploding.

Luke realized he would have to reach down deep to elicit inner strength and fortitude to carry on. His first order of business was to call Chester to apprise him of the sultry developments involving Meredith.

Luke called Chester's cell number. There was a pause before Luke could hear Chester's voice.

"Luke," Chester said, "I have been talking with Meredith. She wanted me to hear from her directly as to the recent problems. You should know she has placed on the record some salacious comments about you, to put it delicately. I need to get back to Meredith and will call you ASAP."

Luke was seething but needed to keep it together.

"OK, Chester," Luke said. "I look forward to hearing from you and bringing you up to speed."

Although Luke was adroit at multitasking, he was incapable of contemplating anything but the anticipated prevarication and obfuscation that Meredith likely had woven in a web of character assassination to cast him as the bad guy.

Luke's intuitive senses told him lobbying for PENA could become the bane of his existence.

Luke hoped Chester would call him within a few minutes. But an hour passed and still no text messages or phone calls from Chester. Luke was getting jumpy, but he resisted the temptation to call Chester for fear he would be perceived as rattled and defensive.

Luke was speaking in soliloquies, which he occasionally did when perplexed. The realization he was talking to himself led to a faint grin as he remembered a conversation many years ago with his mother, Mary.

Mary had told her son it is OK for him to talk to himself but warned not to answer his questions as if he were in a two-way conversation with himself.

Several hours later, Chester's cell number flashed on Luke's phone. Luke took a deep breath and exhaled, then let the phone ring twice before picking up the call.

Chester explained he had intended to call Luke hours ago, but Liz, his wife of thirty-five years, needed to discuss their son's impending wedding.

"When Liz beckons, I respond," Chester said with a laugh. "After all, she is the boss."

How ironic and hypocritical, Luke thought. A catastrophic injury or death itself would be the only reason to excuse Luke from expeditiously responding to Chester. And Luke asked himself how a discussion about a wedding delays a time-sensitive phone call for several hours.

In the immediate moments that followed, Luke either considered Chester an insensitive SOB or an out-of-touch CEO teetering on senility. Or possibly Chester wanted Luke to sweat a bit. As Luke pondered that last thought, he wondered what Chester had up his proverbial sleeve.

Chester was aware the media campaign was crashing and burning, but he did not know the half of it as he was in the dark about the impending implosion of Meredith's fake news stories.

But Luke knew informing Chester about Meredith and the bogus news feeds would be a futile exercise. Regardless of what Meredith did or did not do, Chester held Luke accountable as PENA's leader in the field.

Chester hammered this point home during their phone conversation.

"This is a bottom-line business, and the buck stops with you, period," Chester told Luke.

Luke processed Chester's comment then politely responded, "If I am accountable for everything—the good, bad, and ugly—then empower me to make personnel changes if need be."

Chester interjected at this point, assuming Luke would ask for Meredith to be relieved of her position.

"Luke, why don't you take a few days off to collect your thoughts and get back to me?" suggested Chester. "I don't want to discuss any personnel changes, particularly relating to Meredith."

Chester added that Meredith has filed a complaint, accusing Luke of sexual harassment.

"I am not going to fire a woman at the behest of the man who is accused of sexually harassing her," Chester said in a firm-deft tone.

Luke asked Chester for a copy of the complaint. Chester refused, telling Luke PENA's protocol is to fully conduct an investigation before the alleged harasser received a copy of the complaint.

The two men ended the phone call with the understanding they would follow up within twenty-four hours.

CHAPTER
8

AT CROSSROADS

The next morning, Luke was on a direct flight to Palm Beach. Luke was a fighter, but he knew a lost cause when he saw one. Investing more time, energy, and money into the campaign without a new strategy would be lose-lose.

Luke also recognized he was beaten down, jaded, and missing the mojo and swagger that has given him a competitive advantage. He would need to be in the right frame of mind with a rested body if he were to be resilient in resurrecting a campaign from a postmortem state.

After touching down in Palm Beach at about noon, Luke went to his favorite watering hole, an Irish pub named Lucky Charms.

While taking a gulp of a dark Guinness and waiting for his Reuben sandwich, Luke casually peeked at the big screen television affixed to a corner wall. As he turned away from the television, he asked no one in particular why the television was programmed to a cable news channel in an Irish sports bar.

"Don't you know, Luke, that you still have a half- pint of Irish Catholic blood in you?" Brendan Donnelly, day manager of Lucky Charms, said in his thick Irish brogue. "Reverence, my lad. Our new pope is to be featured on this channel."

Luke leaned over the bar counter and placed his hands in front of his head as if he were bowing and scraping for repentance.

There was a collective groan from Luke's fellow patrons as they processed Brendan's comment. But to a person, each gazed at the television as a news reporter talked about Pope Francis's impending visit to the United States and the release of Evangelii Gaudium (The Joy of the Gospel).

The program cut away from the reporter to show a live news conference in which the pope encouraged former Catholics to return to the church.

It is what Pope Francis said next that captivated Luke. Francis said the church must be welcoming for all who seek the Catholic faith by removing barriers steeped in a small set of narrow rules.

Luke appeared mesmerized as the pope continued. "We are all sinners and are not in a position to judge. We must look beyond our past sins and love one another as Jesus loves us. This will allow us to follow Jesus's model example, nurture our souls, and have a spiritual purpose in our lives."

The pontiff also expounded on respect and dignity for all and implored all to practice humility.

Luke washed down the Guinness, devoured the Reuben, and wondered if listening to the pope's outreach was a carpe diem–type moment for him.

He then remembered his former priest, Fr. Anthony DeMaria, telling him that carpe diem—the here and now—is not merely an arbitrary coincidence. "There are reasons why we are in a specific place at a point in time," Luke recalled Father DeMaria repeatedly saying to him.

Luke told himself, "Father DeMaria could tell me whether the pope's words were cascading to the diocesan and parish levels. I must call him."

After nearly two decades of no contact with Father DeMaria, Luke was calling him on an impulse. This was atypical for Luke, whose modus operandi was to strategize his every move.

Father DeMaria's longtime clerical assistant, Maria Lacasa, answered the call. She explained that Father DeMaria would not have any availability for the balance of the week unless Luke could meet with him today at 3:00 p.m.

Without hesitation, Luke accepted the invitation.

Father DeMaria was the celebrant at Luke and Bethany's wedding at St. Agatha Catholic Church in Lake Worth. Father DeMaria was an associate priest there until he was reassigned to be pastor of Hope Rural Parish, located in a migrant area within the Diocese of Palm Beach.

As Luke drove to Father DeMaria's office, he asked himself what had come over him. Suddenly, the daily issues right in front of his face were on the back burner. For the first time in his adult life, he was beginning to question whether earning the almighty dollar was the be-all and end-all in life.

As Luke introspected, he acknowledged that his home, cars, country club membership, and travel budget did not ensure long-term happiness and eternal life.

He ruminated that something was missing in his life.

Maybe Pope Francis has it right when he conveyed a message about a higher purpose to do God's will, Luke thought.

Or Luke wondered if he were subliminally creating a diversion from his helter-skelter professional life.

Before Luke could cogitate further, he parked in the Hope Rural Parish office lot and entered the building. An austere ambiance pervaded through the office.

Luke beckoned for Maria.

Then Luke heard a voice. "Maria is not here. Can I help you?"

A silver-haired man wearing a roman collar approached from the shadows of a dimly lit room and greeted Luke with open arms. "Good to see you, Luke," Father DeMaria said. "What has it been, twenty or so years?"

Luke responded it has been twenty-three years since he and Father DeMaria squared off in racquetball.

"Oh yes, I remember those games," Father DeMaria said. "They were competitive, and Luke, you were a formidable opponent."

The two men exchanged a handshake, and Father DeMaria gestured for Luke to sit on a chair next to a card table.

"Maria does not work in the afternoons because we do not have the finances to pay her full-time," Father DeMaria explained. "And I refuse to put our precious resources into a building that otherwise can truly help the needy," Father DeMaria replied in an attempt to head off potential questions about a facility in apparent need of renovation.

"Well, Luke, what can I do for you?" Father DeMaria asked, cutting to the chase.

Attempting to be reverent, Luke referred to his former pastor as Father DeMaria.

"Please, Luke," Father DeMaria interjected, "call me Father Tony."

"OK, Tony, I mean Father Tony," Luke said, correcting himself.

"You may know, I am a fallen Catholic," Luke said, trying to lay some sort of predicate to justify why he suddenly asked for a meeting after no contact for so long.

"The other day," Luke continued, "I watched a news report in which Pope Francis encouraged people like me to come back to the church. I would like to know if Pope Francis's sentiments are embraced at the diocesan and parish levels."

Father Tony smiled then said, "I see." Father Tony then paused. The silence was awkward.

And Father Tony's "I see" comment perplexed Luke. What in the hell am I to make of that? Luke thought. Then Father Tony proceeded. "You have asked the key question. He is a godsend. The pontiff's ability to express his joy for all God's people and set a loving and caring tone that can be seen around the world is a contagious blessing. His humility, empathy, and devotion to the poor have connected with the masses."

And then the affable expression on Father Tony's face transformed to a pointed look as he reached for a nearby bookshelf and clutched a newly bound copy of Evangelii Gaudium.

"We can see in this apostolic exhortation the pontiff is unabashed to challenge the rich and powerful that the culture of prosperity has deadened us to the misery of the poor," Father Tony continued. "Corruption, debt, tax evasion, mass layoffs, and environmental degradation all are rebuked."

"Environmental degradation?" Luke asked quizzically.

"My boy," Father Tony said, trying not to sound condescending, "do you not remember the seven themes of Catholic social teaching, including care of God's creation?"

Luke avoided the question by responding with levity, "The church was serious about all of that stuff?"

Father Tony reached for an article on his desk entitled "Catholic Climate Covenant: Care for Creation, Care for the Poor," which was a montage of Pope Francis's quotes about the environment.

Father Tony then read one of the excerpts that pierced through Luke's inner core to his very heart.

"I wish to mention another threat to peace, which arises from the greedy exploitation of environmental resources," Fr. Tony said.

Luke sighed and absorbed the comment. He was in no position to defend his tenuous position as an advocate to make profit to the detriment of the environment.

Father Tony turned his attention to why Luke had requested a meeting.

"Luke, you asked me a very good and serious question a few minutes ago," Father DeMaria said.

"I believe you and your lovely family would be welcomed in any Catholic Church," Father Tony said. "And, Luke, please know there is always an open invitation for the McAlarneys at Hope Rural."

Luke thanked Father Tony as the two men stood and embraced.

"Please give Bethany my best," Father Tony said as Luke exited the parish office.

Luke felt a bounce in his step as if a burgeoning weight around his shoulders were lessening.

On the drive home, he questioned why life had been so complex and, at times, confusing. He wondered if life could be a bit simpler and whether he could actually see the metaphoric forest through the trees.

CHAPTER

9

A NEW DIRECTION

Luke had not heard from Chester and was not about to call him on this day. He wanted to be extricated from all the drama surrounding PENA for at least another day or so.

Another twenty-four to forty-eight hours would allow him to delve into Evangelii Gaudium and reacquaint himself with Catholic social teaching. He also wanted to understand what was transpiring with his conscience.

Luke thought it was odd he was suddenly having internal struggles about values, priorities, and behaviors. It was almost as if his conscience had become awakened after so many years in dormancy in which his approach to win at all costs and his devotion to false gods of material wealth were not questioned.

Luke wondered whether his feelings of guilt were subliminal messages recessed in his psyche from experiences as a child. Or borrowing Sigmund Freud's psychology playbook, he theorized if the part of his mind that was altruistic was pushing back against the part to satisfy primal and hedonistic needs.

And finally, Luke did not rule out the possibility he was undergoing a spiritual transformation.

Whatever was happening, Luke believed it to be life changing. He was questioning the hand that fed him. He was a hired gun. Pay him well, and he would deliver the goods.

There were no mental gymnastics in which he would discern right or wrong, good versus evil, and the long-term impact of his successful lobbying efforts.

His mantra was repeating a message until it was accepted as the unadulterated truth.

One of Luke's lobbying rules was never equivocate.

But now he wanted to understand the compelling interest, if there was one, to preserve natural resources.

Luke did not know why, but he was growing a conscience. And he suddenly had an aversion to prevaricators, charlatans, and anyone who accumulates wealth to the detriment of the common good.

He returned to Lucky Charms and surfed such environmental websites as Green Peace, Preserving Mother Earth, and God's Creation.

Although each of the websites posted a video with a voiceover nuanced in a distinct parlance, the messaging drove home the same point: the onus is on human beings to be caretakers of the planet for posterity.

Luke sat at the table in a contrite state, not knowing where to begin to ask for forgiveness.

In some respects, he wanted to be dismissive of the environmental material as propaganda. But an inner voice was telling him the messages rang pure and true.

A website entitled "The Making of a Well-Formed Conscience" piqued his interest. He read case studies of several subjects. One such subject reminded Luke of himself. In that study, a middle-aged man had begun questioning much of what he did in his professional and personal life. He had undergone a sudden introspection in which his primal needs of hedonism were no longer superseding the values and morals that were inculcated into his conscience at a young age. His value system of honesty and living by the Golden Rule were fighting back, probably triggered by an episode in which he was forced to confront a behavior that was contrary to his upbringing.

As Luke absorbed the case study, he applied it to his recent experiences.

I have never been one for psychobabble, Luke thought, but this may explain what is happening to me.

Luke knew his crash course in a well-formed conscience needed to end, at least for the time being. He realized PENA is his livelihood, and the last time he checked, he was in the middle of a PR crisis.

CHAPTER

10

PREPARING FOR THE INEVITABLE CONFRONTATION

Luke perused his voicemail messages. There were no messages from Chester.

Actually, Luke was relieved he did not have to interact with Chester.

Time away from him, Meredith, PENA's board of directors, and everyone else associated with the campaign was welcome relief.

But no communication from the boss for nearly seventy-two hours in the midst of a crisis made no sense to Luke. The radio silence not only made Luke uneasy but also downright paranoid.

No communication from Chester, whom Luke considered enigmatic, was beyond the bounds of rational explanation.

"Is Chester setting me up?" Luke asked himself, sounding more paranoid by the moment.

Luke decided to end the speculation and called Chester. Much to Luke's surprise, Chester answered the call on the first ring.

"I have been waiting for you to call, Luke," Chester said. "I have asked the board to convene at my office tomorrow, and you should be here too."

The combination of a directive and the casualness in which Chester spoke was perplexing. But Luke was in no position to stir things up and said, "Chester, you can count on me. I will be there."

Luke asked if preparation was needed for the meeting.

"I don't know what to tell you, Luke," Chester said in a weary voice. "The board is not pleased. I expect them to take the gloves off in their assessment of you and the PR campaign."

Luke was not surprised Chester had detached himself from the imploding campaign, presumably to be insulated from rebuke.

In Luke's view, Chester was not much different from the politicos who were quick to take credit for whatever bodes well and deflect any potential calamity onto convenient scapegoats.

At this moment in time, there was no question Luke was one of Chester's scapegoats. Luke had been blindsided, but he should have seen it coming.

His uncanny knack to anticipate next moves had betrayed him. Then again, the thought of a derailing PR campaign and Chester playing the blame game had not been in Luke's house of cards.

The best advice Chester had given Luke was to get a good-night's rest and bring his A game to tomorrow's meeting.

As the two men ended their phone call, Luke immediately booked a flight scheduled to depart from Palm Beach in just three hours. He would have to move quickly.

He stopped at his home in a rush to pack an overnight bag. As he headed to his upstairs bedroom, Corey and Bree both saw their dad.

Corey gave Bree a nudge as if it were her cue to renew her conversation about the trip to Jamaica.

"Dad, you have not been available to talk about the trip with my friends," Bree said, attempting to lay the groundwork for her dad's acquiescence. "So I told them I can go."

"How much will the trip cost, and who will you be staying with?" Luke asked.

Bree said airfare is $2,000, which she would have to pay. But she said her friends would provide hotel accommodations and much of the food.

Luke was unsettled about the trip and said, "Bree, I have to catch a flight in less than three hours. This conversation will have to wait until I return from New York."

But Bree insisted she has to schedule flight reservations immediately.

Luke relented. "It is OK with me if it is OK with your mother." Bethany then shot Luke a look that could kill.

"This is your dad's decision," Bethany said, "but I think this is crazy."

Bree was ecstatic. "Thanks, Mom and Dad. You're are the greatest."

Bree would be heading to Jamaica without disclosing to her parents that her traveling friends were mostly young adult males who would be paying for her living expenses, including overnight accommodations.

CHAPTER

11

LUKE'S STRATEGY

Luke's flight touched down at LaGuardia a few minutes before midnight. He located a cabbie who transported him to a hotel that was walking distance from PENA's headquarters.

Luke asked for a wakeup call at 5:00 a.m. He wanted to have plenty of time to shower, dress, and collect his thoughts for the 9:00 a.m. board meeting.

As Luke's head hit the pillow, his body was tired, but his mind was transfixed with thoughts and prospective questions that board members would be asking. He barely caught a wink of sleep when the phone rang for the wakeup call.

Luke thought, "What the hell, I might as well get this day started."

Luke stood in the shower for twenty minutes, allowing the warm water to shoot jets of spray to his sore muscles and achy bones.

Showering always had been a safe haven for Luke. The rush of water hitting his flesh was not only therapeutic but also allowed him to do some of his best thinking to problem solve.

Showering also was a refuge for him as life appeared to slow down and challenges often were reduced to their most simplistic form.

But on this morning, there was no panacea and nary a eureka moment.

Luke walked to the bedroom mirror and asked himself what he was about to do. He had butterflies in his stomach and felt like a bundle of nerves.

He clutched the St. Christopher necklace around his neck and kissed it. He then donned his power navy blue suit, combed his hair, and picked up his briefcase.

As Luke turned to exit the hotel room, a quote from German author Johann Wolfgang von Goethe mentally flashed from the deep recesses of his mind to the frontal lobe of his immediate thoughts: "Never allow what matters most to be at the mercy of what matters least."

That thought, at least for the moment, gave Luke what he needed most—the fortitude to square off against Chester and the PENA board on his terms and in his version of Custer's Last Stand.

As he arrived at PENA, Luke was in no mood to engage in levity and make small talk with Chester's executive assistant, Lindsay, or anyone else for that matter.

He checked in with a receptionist in PENA's waiting room and remained standing as he took inventory of his phone and text messages. While doing so, several board members walked though the waiting room to Chester's office as if they owned the place.

Luke nodded to Billy Joe, Marvin Rothenstein, and newly appointed board members Daniel Ginilotti and Albert Henrique as they walked with a purpose. Billy Joe placed his right hand above his shoulder in a perfunctory wave as he passed by Luke. Marvin turned his head to make eye contact with Luke as he followed the others in a procession.

Luke remained in the waiting room. He assumed Chester and the board were engaged in last moment discussions.

After a few anxious minutes, the receptionist signaled for Luke, stating, "Mr. Ferguson and the board will see you, Mr. McAlarney."

As Luke walked into Chester's office, he felt unsure and unsettled. There was no bounce in his step. His self-confident swagger and moxie were missing.

Chester, standing behind his desk as if it were a fortress, said, "Luke, you know Billy Joe and Marvin." Luke nodded and smiled, attempting to be as pleasant as possible.

But Chester added, "You have not met Mr. Ginolotti and Mr. Henrique," both of whom approached Luke to shake his hand.

Maybe the new board members will give me a fair hearing, Luke thought.

But without warning, Billy Joe chimed in. "Chester, screw the formalities. Let's get to the bottom line."

"Billy Joe is right," Chester said. "Time is of the essence."

Then Chester ambushed Luke with his latest bombshell. "I received a phone call late last night from Randolph Frost, one of the executives of OWL. Several of the reporters whom Luke and Meredith hired to provide video news feeds to OWL are acknowledging they are not reporters and read from fabricated news scripts.

"OWL is attempting to contain this story, but if it gets in the hands of the national media, OWL is going to point the accusatory finger at us," Chester said.

BUILDING A CONSCIENCE

Luke was not surprised. He had not shared his recent conversation with U.S. Senator Belue, who had a conversation with Mr. Frost about the fabricated news stories.

The senator told Luke that news of the scandal is infiltrating the Senate. He intimated that if the scandal were to be promulgated, favorable passage of SR 538 would be unlikely.

Senator Belue confided in Luke the scandal was rumored to be linked to sources affiliated with Congressman Reynolds' office.

"Of course, it makes perfect sense because the odious Bobby Reynolds and his dilettante, Jerry Butler, were never far from where trouble was brewing," Luke said to himself.

It did not take a rocket scientist to piece together a connection between Congressman Reynolds and Meredith, who has not talked with Luke since her nude folly in Steele City.

Luke then focused on the immediacy as Billy Joe approached him and leaned in so they were inches apart.

"What do you have to say for yourself, Luke?" Billy Joe asked. "You were in charge of this operation."

Luke stepped backward to put some distance between him and Billy Joe. As he prepared to respond,

Billy Joe continued his diatribe. "I am not interested in what you have to say. I just have one question for you. Can you fix this?"

Luke had a thick skin and did not scare easily. He could read Billy Joe like a book. Billy Joe's strategy was intended to shame and intimidate Luke into doing whatever was necessary to make the fabricated news stories go away and put the PR campaign back on track.

Luke decided he would play along with Billy Joe.

"By fixing this," Luke answered, "you mean whatever means possible to extinguish a scandal by possibly engaging in fraud, conspiracy, blackmail, slander, and libel?"

"We pay you to take care of everything—hook, line, and sinker," Billy Joe emphatically said as his veins flexed from his neck.

Luke paused, knowing Billy Joe's indignation gave him the self-imposed right for subversive fury.

Then Luke stated, "I see. It was my understanding I was hired to lobby for favorable passage of the pipeline and then facilitate a public relations campaign to seal the deal. But it appears that you, Mr. Payne, and this board are adding organized crime to my job description."

Luke said he is unsure how many people know about the fake news stories, which were created without his knowledge and approval. "And Chester," Luke added, "has kept on payroll the person who is responsible for the fiasco."

Luke's comment elicited the ire of Chester.

"Luke, you are venturing into dangerous territory," Chester warned. "If you continue discussing another employee, then I will have to disclose the salacious allegations against you."

Chester obviously was dangling sexual harassment allegations against Luke to discredit him and, in doing so, force him to retreat into abashed capitulation.

Luke had a strong intuitive sense that Chester had briefed the board about the sordid saga in which Meredith implicated Luke.

"Chester, don't stop on my account," Luke said. "I have nothing to hide."

Chester looked at Luke then to Billy Joe and Marvin and said, "I will not turn our board meetings into a Peyton Place of she-said and he-said."

"Very good, Chester," Luke said sardonically. Luke then attempted to address Billy Joe's question. "To cover up felonious activity is of itself a crime. To do as Mr. Payne has implored me to do would involve possible conspiracy and shake down our friends and foes in the form of bribes, blackmail, and other forms of not so subtle intimidation."

Chester responded, "That will be quite enough, Luke. No one here is asking you to commit crimes."

"Fine," Luke said, "but could Mr. Payne be specific when he demands that I clean up the mess?"

Chester, in his attempt to be the good cop, approached Luke and put his arms around him.

"We have been friends for a long time. Each of us has your back. We expect you to defuse the problems."

Marvin approached Luke and stated with sagacious condescension, "I've always admired your ability to persevere and come out on top."

Marvin patted Luke on the back and added, "Hang in there. We have confidence in you. Bring this thing in for a landing."

Luke was prepared for Billy Joe's incendiary interrogation and bad-cop act. But Chester and Marvin ingratiating themselves as the good cops had caught Luke off guard. They were playing to his reputed strength to persevere as the survivor—a survivor of the fittest.

But Luke had changed. He was having an internal conflict with what to do. It was no longer as simple as fighting the good fight. There was honor in walking away if spurious and insidious means were PENA's calling card.

Luke then responded with a proposal, "I will piece together a strategic plan to clean up the campaign and forward to each of you as board members. The board can accept the proposal as is or amend as it deems necessary. I then will carry out the board's approved plan."

Luke thought he had them between a rock and a hard place. That board wanted the campaign to be extricated from scandal and to move forward.

But it became apparent the board did not want to be complicit in how Luke cleaned up the mess.

Chester, speaking on behalf of the board, said the proposal is atypical of how PENA does business.

"PENA always has given you autonomy to maneuver in the public policy arena to make expedient decisions that serve all of us well," Chester said. "You have earned our trust."

Luke thanked Chester and the board for the trust they had bestowed on him and added, "These are not ordinary times in which our typical practices are to be applied. Metaphorically speaking in a maritime context, we are in unchartered waters and our ship is in distress. This situation necessitates an SOS in which all of us are onboard and equally protected and culpable."

But the board was having none of the "one for all and all for one," refusing to capitulate as it held an impregnable line of defense.

Chester turned to Luke and said, "You are trying to change the rules in midstream, and that is simply a nonstarter."

Luke replied, "Each of you know I see things to the end. That is what I do. I came here today in good faith to reconcile and agree to a plan of action that all of us can live with."

Luke took a deep breath and then exhaled. He appeared calm on the exterior, but inside, he could hear his heart pulsating as if there were an inner voice telling him to get out before he lost his self-respect and dignity. He was looking for an exit strategy.

The challenge of addressing the fake news stories and placing the PR campaign on track was part of it. But the other piece in play was Luke no longer had the passion to be a part of something that undermined creation.

Luke then scanned the faces of Chester, the board, and said, "I want to clean up the mess, but this will be no easy matter. I honestly do not know what it will take to get this thing back on track. But I do know it will necessitate giving some people what they want in order to guarantee their silence."

Billy Joe turned to Chester and interjected, "Your boy has the audacity to be angling for more money."

Chester looked at Luke and said, "We might be able to accommodate a pay raise if you can get us through these rough spots in the immediate future."

Luke replied, "A few weeks ago, I would have jumped at that offer. But this is no longer about money. This is about me living with my conscience."

Billy Joe again looked at Chester and yelped, "Your boy Luke has gotten soft."

Luke turned to Billy Joe. "You call it getting soft, but I call it living with my conscience."

Marvin intervened and said, "I think we have reached a point of diminishing return. Right, Chester?"

Chester looked downward and nodded. At that moment, Luke and PENA's relationship was indelibly severed.

As Luke picked up his briefcase and began exiting the office, Chester said, "Luke, know that if you leave now under these circumstances, there will never be an opportunity to return to PENA. You will be leaving for life."

Luke turned and gazed at Chester. "I know," he quipped with a wink and nod.

Chester, standing behind his desk, called PENA's security. Luke could hear Chester stating, "Please send security to my office to escort Mr. McAlarney from the building."

As Chester put down the phone, Luke responded, "That really is not necessary."

Chester replied, "On the contrary, Mr. McAlarney. It is very necessary."

It was necessary because Chester wanted to openly humiliate Luke as an example of an unabashed, ungrateful, and incorrigible employee who has the gall to repudiate PENA.

Within moments, two burly security guards entered the office as Chester pointed to Luke.

One security guard grabbed Luke by his left arm. The other security guard snatched his briefcase and gave it to Chester, who pulled out the contents.

Luke was handed the empty briefcase and then forcibly escorted past Lindsay's desk for all to see. As they approached the exit door, both security guards gave Luke a swift push in the back as the door automatically opened, and Luke stumbled onto the sidewalk.

CHAPTER
12

LUKE'S NEXT STEP

Luke straightened his tie, collected himself, and murmured, "Well, I don't have a job, but at least I have my self-respect."

He was trying to affirm what he had done.

He told himself, "This is the first day of the rest of my life."

As Luke began to wave for a taxi, he saw a homeless man standing on the sidewalk.

Luke proactively approached the man and asked if he were hungry. The man, with shoulder-length hair, a full beard, and wearing a T-shirt and jeans permeated with holes and ripped as if he were wearing rags, nodded with an audible yes.

Luke handed the man a $20 bill and asked where he sleeps. The man looked down as if he were embarrassed and answered in broken English, "Wherever I can.

Sometimes in a nearby park and at the Salvation Army and YMCA when I can get in."

"Are you treated well at the YMCA and Salvation Army?" Luke asked. The man, not sure where Luke's line of questioning was going, hesitated and answered, "Ya, they are good to me when I am allowed to stay with them."

Luke asked where the Salvation Army was located. The man pointed to the corner and began to walk in that direction. Luke followed.

As the men arrived at the Salvation Army, Luke extended his hand to the man and said, "My name is Luke." The man answered, "You can call me Carlos."

Once inside, Luke asked for some handout materials about the Salvation Army. He read about SA's mission to serve the poor by offering food, shelter, clothing, and basic medical care from nursing staff.

Luke inquired if the Salvation Army could provide Carlos with extended overnight accommodations.

A petite elderly female volunteer, whose dark hair was permeated in gray, stood behind a counter as she summoned for the daytime manager to find out if Carlos can receive a bed for this evening.

In a few moments, the manager, a middle-aged, portly-looking woman named Agatha, appeared. She greeted Luke and Carlos with a smile and said, "The problem is we do not have enough beds for all of the people who want to stay here. But we will make every effort for Carlos to have a bed for tonight."

"If I contribute $1,000, would that guarantee a few more beds for Carlos and other guests?" Luke asked. Agatha responded, "It certainly would help."

Luke handed Agatha his debit card to deduct the contribution from his bank account.

Luke asked Agatha for her business card and promised to follow up to check on Carlos in the immediate future.

As Luke began to leave, Carlos turned to him and said, "What you do for the least of our brothers and sisters you do for Jesus."

Luke looked at Carlos and responded, "Everything we have is from the grace of God."

In short order, Luke flagged down a cab. As he was traveling to the airport, he contemplated the irony that when he was lucratively and gainfully employed, he did little to help the poor. Now that he is unemployed, he is more giving.

On the flight back home, Luke agonized how to break the news to Bethany about his termination from PENA.

CHAPTER

13

TROUBLE ON THE HOME FRONT

When Luke arrived home, he greeted Bethany and said, "I have something to tell you." Bethany responded, "There is something you need to know."

Luke said, "OK, you first."

Bethany said Bree's little adventure to Jamaica was the trip from hell. Luke looked puzzled. Bethany stared at him and asked, "You remember, Luke, the trip you approved without asking her whom she was traveling with and why her so-called friends were willing to pay for her accommodations in Jamaica?"

Luke was attempting to understand, realizing Bethany had repressed feelings about Bree's trip and needed to vent her frustrations. He also wanted to defuse a potential argument, particularly before sharing the news about his unemployment status.

But Luke could not resist a slight verbal jab. "Well, Bethany, the way I remember it, you were minimally complicit with the trip."

Bethany retorted, "Don't play the blame game, Luke. You are her father. As usual, my opinion did not seem to carry much weight."

Luke said, "OK, Bethany, let's dispense with who has the familial decision making and who does not. Just tell me what happened."

First, Bethany said, "You should know Bree was only one of two girls who made the trip with five boys."

"Are you kidding me?" Luke asked. Bethany replied, "I would not kid about such a thing."

Luke interjected, "Please tell me this story ends well."

"Luke," Bethany said, "the good news is Bree returned home unscathed physically. The bad news, well, let's just say the vacation is a living hell."

Bethany continued. "Bree's account of the sordid developments began with her, the boys, and the other girl, Vera, partying in a Jacuzzi. The girls were cajoled to take off their tops and did so.

"The boys snapped pictures of the girls with their phones and vowed that the risqué shots were for their eyes only.

"Can you believe our daughter was so naive to believe that?" Bethany asked in disbelief.

Bethany said Bree told her the party transitioned from the Jacuzzi to a semiprivate beach for hotel guests. The boys asked the girls to remove their bikinis and again promised that the pictures were only for them.

"According to Bree, Vera, without hesitation, stripped nude on the beach," Bethany said. As Bethany continued describing the sultry saga, Luke began to seethe.

Bethany clenched Luke's hand then proceeded. "The boys and Vera exhorted Bree to do the same. Bree reluctantly removed both pieces of her bikini, giving the boys the show they wanted.

"As both girls were standing on the white packed beach in all their glory, the boys asked them to frolic together. The pictures left little to the imagination."

Luke interjected, asking how she knew this.

Bethany explained she had seen the pictures.

Anticipating Luke's next question, Bethany said the boys disseminated the pictures to friends. Images of Bree and Vera have gone viral.

Bethany said Vera's mother contacted her. One of her friends saw pictures on an Instagram account.

Luke asked to see the pictures. Bethany gave a flash drive to Luke, which contained the pictures she had received from Vera's mother.

As Luke perused the pictures, he noticed that Bree had a Cupid arrow tattooed on her left breast and a heart-shaped red tattoo on her lower back. Much to his surprise, Bree had no suntan lines.

Luke turned to Bethany and asked, "Do you know if the tattoos and au natural suntan occurred before or during the Jamaican trip?"

Bethany said she asked Bree that very question, and she simply said, "Jamaica."

Luke wiped perspiration from his brow as he tried to make sense of it all.

"Assuming Bree is telling the truth, the tattoos must have preceded the sunbathing pictures at the private beach," Luke said. "Evidently, we are not getting the whole story."

Luke could not wrap his head around the fact that his little girl recklessly placed herself in harm's way. He knew the family would be shamed by the ubiquitous dissemination of the salacious pictures as people had their say.

Luke knew that people—from the self-anointed righteous to the rank-and-file gossipers, to reprobated opportunists—could be unbelievably cruel and insensitive.

As a father, Luke would have to prepare for the jokes and sneers behind his back. But he realized as humbling as this would be for him and Bethany, this was about making sure Bree could move forward in life. This would be difficult, particularly in the short-term, as Bree would be stigmatized with all the unbecoming words associated with a young girl who shows her body to the world.

Bethany said Bree has been a recluse, cordoning off her bedroom from the rest of the family for the past three days.

"Well, it is time we speak to her," Luke said.

Bethany and Luke walked to her bedroom door, which was locked. They asked her to open the door. After several minutes, Bree eased the door open and walked to her bed.

Much to Luke and Bethany's astonishment, Bree was dressed in a long-sleeved sweater and full-length jeans even though the AC thermostat in their home was set at seventy-eight degrees to offset the summer heat.

Except for her face, every part of her body was covered.

Her eyes were bloodshot from crying and from a dearth of sleep.

Luke tenderly approached Bree and held her hand.

"Together, we will get through this," he said.

Bree hugged her father with the tenacity of a middle linebacker. She clung to him with the hope that he would somehow make everything alright.

As Bree embraced her father, she whispered, "Please take me away from here and Montgomery. There is no way I can go back to that school."

Bethany overheard Bree's comment, and she responded, "We can't run from this. We will have to see it through."

Bree then handed her phone to her mother.

"Look at the hundreds of text messages calling me every name imaginable and asking me to do things that are unspeakable," Bree said tearfully, choking back sobs.

While Bree showered and got a bite to eat, Bethany told Luke that Bree's mental state is in the throes of fragility and, as such, is in need of psychotherapy and counseling services.

Luke hesitated then asked, "Are you sure she needs this? I pose the question because we may not be in a position to pay for services at this point in time."

Bethany took umbrage with Luke's quip about money.

"Damn it, Luke, quit worrying about money," Bethany said. "We are talking about our daughter. Her welfare must come first."

Luke tried to truncate a conversation about money and asked Bethany if she knew the names of the boys who accompanied Bree on the trip.

"I am working on it," Bethany said tersely. "Good," Luke said, "because there are legal penalties for disseminating nude pictures of minors."

"Luke, I want those boys to be held accountable, but we don't know all of the facts yet, and our attention should be focused on Bree to ensure she is of a sound mental and emotional state," Bethany said.

Bethany approached Luke and hugged him.

"Thank you for being here, Luke," she said as

tears welled in her eyes. "I could not deal with this without you."

Luke wrapped his arms around her waist and said, "I always will be here for you, Bethany. Together, we can get through this."

Bethany said Bree needs their support now more than ever.

"Call it mother's intuition, but it is imperative Bree receives counseling from a highly regarded therapist who can get her though this," Bethany said.

Luke retorted, "I hear you, Bethany. There is no doubt she is in a state of fragility. "It is just that I . . . I don't know what we can afford."

Bethany was aghast and her mouth opened, but nary a word spewed from her lips. Her eyes pierced directly at Luke.

She then said with a hue and cry in her voice, "You ought to be ashamed of yourself, placing money over the welfare of our daughter. Therapeutic interventions may save her from debilitating into a manic depressive state and all that comes with it."

Bethany's voice trailed off. She could not bring herself to say the unthinkable—Bree is potentially suicidal.

She composed herself and then continued. "Honestly, Luke, sometimes I neither understand you nor do I know you."

Luke knew he had to tell her about his jobless status.

"Bethany," Luke said, "you know I would do anything for you and the kids. It is just . . . just that . . . we have been living paycheck to paycheck, and now I do not have a paycheck."

Bethany, not believing what she had heard, asked, "What are you talking about, Luke?"

Luke was visibly unsettled, unsure what to say and how Bethany would respond. He knew Bree's situation, coupled with his unemployment, would be more than Bethany could handle.

Luke looked downward, unable to make eye contact with Bethany, who had been seated on the couple's bed but stood and placed her hands on her hips and said, "I am waiting for an answer."

Luke knew she was right. She deserved an honest answer.

"It is like this," Luke said. "Chester and the board terminated me because I was unwilling to clean up a mess that would have likely led to me engaging in illegal, immoral, and unethical behavior."

Bethany asked, "Since when did you become such a choirboy, Luke?"

Before Luke could respond, she asked whether he had a choice to remain in his position or whether he was fired.

Luke exhaled then said, "I would be employed if I had no conscience and was willing to do whatever means were necessary to win the PR battle to install the pipeline."

Contemplating Luke's response at face value, Bethany knew her husband allowed himself to be fired and did so with little or no regard for his family.

She then heard herself saying the following words, "Luke, I get it that you have been the breadwinner in the family and, as such, make most of our financial decisions. But did the thought occur to you that I should have been consulted before you decided that satisfying your conscience superseded everything else?"

Luke had been attempting to curry empathy from Bethany. But she was having none of it. The more he talked, the angrier she became.

Luke realized this, but in an act of desperation, he tried to win her over. "Bethany, don't think for a moment I went into the meeting with Chester and the board with a premeditation to be fired. I had no idea how the conversation would unfold."

Luke told Bethany he did not anticipate an ultimatum from PENA.

"It was not as if I could leave the meeting and consult with you," Luke told her. "I rejected an ultimatum that would have entangled me into PENA's insidious web. I could not continue at PENA under those circumstances and be the husband and father you and the kids deserve."

Bethany's forehead was strewn with a wrinkle—the type that becomes visible when she was on mental overload.

Bethany was an intelligent woman, but she could not mentally connect with Luke's newfound sensibilities and active state of conscience. She slowly shook her head as if she were in disbelief and in a state of hopelessness.

Luke sensed she needed a lifeline for her to have some semblance of hope for the future.

"We do have assets—the home, cars, and yacht," Luke said. "They could be liquidated and get us through the rough patches in the foreseeable future."

But he cautioned liquidating assets is usually time-consuming and not conducive for immediate cash flow needs.

This prompted Bethany to ask, "How do we pay for Bree to get the help that she needs?"

Luke responded with a blank stare but approached her and said, "We will figure out a way."

But Bethany pushed Luke away, saying, "You find a way, and then I will be approachable. Until then, keep your distance."

Luke was visibly shaken as he backpedaled a few steps, giving Bethany space.

Bethany rubbed her forehead as if she had an excruciating headache. She was weary and on the brink of defeat.

She looked as if she were a picture of utter despair.

Her head swirled with myopic thoughts as she was in a vertiginous state of mind.

Bethany was in no condition to decide anything in this moment in time.

But she yearned for a semblance of control in her life, which suddenly had been turned upside down in discombobulation.

She audibly sighed then cathartically said to her husband, "Luke, I need time to figure things out."

He nodded animatedly and said he will support her in any way that he can.

But Luke was unprepared for Bethany's next request. "What I need you to do Luke is give me space. I need peace, quiet, and space from you."

Luke responded, "What are you saying, Bethany?"

She was attempting to be as tactful as possible under the circumstances but decided to be direct.

"I need you to move out, at least for a while," she said.

Her last comment gave Luke a sick feeling as if his body had been robbed of all vitality.

Luke was in a total state of despair, but he managed to find the words to force Bethany to consider the ramification of her directive.

"Call it what it really is," Luke said. "This is a breakup."

He then abruptly stepped toward Bethany as the muscles tightened in his face, and he balled up his right fist.

Bethany stooped down and covered her head in a defensive position.

Luke then stopped, turned on his heels, and walked to the closet, where he hastily threw a few of his clothes and other belongings into a small bag.

Luke had never been in such an ambivalent state—apoplectic and hurt. He did not want to stay where he was not welcome and his only thought was to get the hell out of there as quickly as possible.

He briskly walked down the stairs with the sole purpose to exit through the front door with maximum celerity. But Corey and Bree had heard their parents arguing and stood at the front door as an impediment for their father's impending exit.

Both Corey and Bree asked their father where he was going.

Luke, as he reached for the doorknob, responded in a stentorian voice, "Excuse me."

Luke looked at the kids and added, "Ask your mother that question."

The kids appeared startled and moved aside as their father whisked by them.

They watched as Luke threw his overnight bag into the Jaguar and shifted the car into gear as he peeled out of the driveway.

CHAPTER 14

LUKE THE ENVIRONMENTALIST

As Luke sped south on I-95, he called Lindsay Garmin to find out how much back pay would be electronically deposited in his checking account in the coming weeks.

Lindsay said she prepared a final pay statement within hours after Luke's resignation per Chester's directive.

Luke corrected Lindsay. "I did not resign. I was fired."

Lindsay said Chester was very clear as he indicated to classify Luke's departure as a resignation.

"Of course," Luke told himself. "Chester does not want PENA to have to pay unemployment compensation."

Lindsay added, "Mr. Ferguson said he wanted to review the paperwork before any checks were processed and forwarded to you, Luke. I don't know if Mr. Ferguson will make any changes, but my summary indicated you would receive one more full paycheck and any unused vacation time as well as information about your pension."

Luke thanked Lindsay for her assistance.

"You are welcome, Luke, but I could lose my job if Mr. Ferguson found out I was talking with you."

Luke replied, "I understand, Lindsay. I will not put you in this situation again."

As the call ended, Luke knew expecting money from PENA was like fool's gold. He always had known that his relationship with PENA was tenuous at best. His relationship with Chester was his job security. Chester could terminate Luke without cause because there was no contractual relationship.

"Chester and PENA were not fair before the breakup, so what possible motivation would they have as a bastion of mercenary thought to be fair and decent at this point?" Luke asked himself.

Luke exited from the interstate and parked at a convenience store. He had nearly $100 cash in his wallet and a credit card with $2,000 available credit. Over the next few weeks, the small sum of cash and the credit card would be his financial lifeline.

Although he had a debit card, he knew Bethany would need every penny in the checking and saving accounts to make ends meet.

Luke topped off the fuel tank of the Jaguar as he pondered his next move. He was wound tight and bursting at the proverbial seams in the aftermath of his extrication from Bethany and the kids. He needed to decompress, and getting the hell out of dodge came readily to mind.

But he did not want to be a heedless wanderer devoid of direction or purpose. However, he did want to escape from the world in which he lived, at least provisionally.

He needed a waypoint. Then it came to him. There is no better way to escape than to enjoy camping, fishing, and boating in the backcountry.

Luke headed toward Alligator Alley en route to Everglades City, home of a Native American reservation, a campground, and a tour guide who led backcountry tours by kayak.

The cabins were austere—one bunk, a stove, and sink. No television or telephone. The bathrooms and showers were walking distance from the cabins. But more importantly, the room rate of $39 was affordable for an unemployed lobbyist with cash flow issues.

The following morning, Luke was purchasing a few staples at a nearby general store and saw an attractive middle-aged woman donning a T-shirt with the caption: "The Everglades is in Florida, but out of this world!"

Luke approached the woman and said with a half smile, "I like your T-shirt, but how do you know the Everglades is out of this world?"

The woman ignored Luke's somewhat veiled attempt at humor. She boomeranged his question back at him. "Your question is like asking Crocodile Dundee about the Outback. I am the local tour guide, kayaking into the Everglades twice a day."

Luke introduced himself and extended his hand. They shook hands while the woman responded, "I am Maggie Sinclair. Pleased to meet you."

Maggie, who spoke with a southern accent affirming her magnanimous South Carolina charm, had short coiffed blond hair. She looked like she could be a cover girl for Women's Health Magazine. She sported a sans-makeup look. Her T-shirt and shorts accentuated her physically fit body, particularly her arms and legs that were nicely toned from the miles of paddling and peddling a kayak each day.

Luke asked Maggie how he could retain her services for a kayaking tour. Maggie reached into her purse and pulled out a card.

"Here," she said, handing her card to Luke. "Call me, and we can schedule a tour."

Luke looked at the card as if he were studying a fact sheet then redirected his gaze with eagerness in his voice. "I will be sure to call."

Maggie replied that she looked forward to hearing from Luke.

But she added, "Just so you know, kayaking in the backcountry is a close and personal encounter of wild and dangerous alligators, pythons, and other reptiles."

Maggie winked at Luke and added, "If you are looking to go beyond your comfort level, call me. But if you are looking for a little R&R, you might want to head to the coastal beaches."

True to his word, Luke followed up, contacting Maggie. They agreed to meet at the landing, 7:00 a.m. sharp. Luke was perspiring profusely as he arrived a few minutes early. The Florida sun already was searing as the air temperature was ninety-plus degrees. The temperature actually felt more intense when considering the high humidity.

Maggie greeted Luke and held a canteen in each hand and asked, "Would you be so kind to fill the canteens at the water pump next to the storage unit?"

Luke scanned the terrain, located the water pump, and filled the canteens as Maggie had requested.

As Luke approached her, she tossed a tube of sunscreen in his direction. After he plucked it from the air, she said, "Rub the sunscreen on all exposed skin and then see me about insect repellant. You will need to put the repellant on the same exposed areas."

Luke did as he was told and then asked, "How in the world are both of us going to fit in the kayak?"

She replied, somewhat peeved by his naiveté as she tersely said, "We won't fit, Luke. That is why each of us has a kayak."

"Oh, I see," said Luke as if he were privy to a sudden revelation. "These are one-man kayaks."

Maggie corrected him and said they are "one- person kayaks."

Luke smiled and retorted, "Of course the female tour guide in the Everglades is an ardent feminist."

She glared at him but said nothing.

Maggie led the way, but Luke kept his kayak directly behind hers. Although he manifested a fearless bravado when interacting with Maggie, he was privately a little unsettled and intimidated about the experience.

Maggie was his security blanket for the tour. There was no way he was going to lose sight of her.

They were paddling from one meandering tributary to another, and in doing so, Luke was completely disoriented. He would have to place blind trust in Maggie that she knew where they were in a maze of barely navigable waterways and how to return to their point of departure.

Along the way, Maggie had pointed to several snakes slithering in the shallows and a couple of alligators sunning themselves on an embankment.

As Luke marveled at the pristine beauty of the Everglades, he wondered how many years it would survive.

Luke reflected on his question as the two kayaks made a ninety-degree turn into an estuary. Suddenly and without provocation, a gator that looked longer than the length of the twelve-foot kayaks aggressively swam toward them.

As the gator approached the kayaks, Maggie attempted to fend off the large reptile with a paddle. The gator did not shy away.

Maggie yelled to Luke, "I will try to preoccupy the gator. Get out of here, now!"

Luke frantically paddled then stopped and turned his head. The gator had rammed Maggie's kayak. The impact forced Maggie overboard.

As she was standing in waist-deep water and several feet from her capsized kayak, the gator submerged. Luke was horrified. He knew in moments the gator would try to pull Maggie below the surface.

Luke's hands were paddling and feet were peddling back to Maggie. As he was within a foot of Maggie, he reached for her hand. They locked hands as Luke tried to pull her into his kayak.

Her upper torso was in the kayak, but her legs were dangling in the water.

As a veteran tour guide, Maggie was calm, but she knew her life was in great peril. She detached a flare gun from the holster appended to her belt and handed it to Luke.

"If the gator attempts to pull me under, aim the flare gun at his head and fire," she hastily said.

No sooner than the words had left Maggie's mouth, her body was being pulled from the kayak.

Luke panicked. He tried to tug on Maggie's arms in an effort to keep her in the kayak. But Luke's brawn was no match for the gator.

He could feel his hands slipping from Maggie's fingers. In a split second, he let go of Maggie's hands and fired the flare gun, aiming directly between the gator's eyes.

Luke stood frozen, not knowing his next step. Thankfully, the flare had hit its mark, and the gator's death grip on Maggie's legs was no more.

The gator, with a powder burn in its head, was injured but alive to retreat and live for another day.

As Luke placed Maggie into the kayak, he could see blood oozing from bite marks on her legs.

Luke began to dial 911, but Maggie grabbed the phone.

"I am trying to save your life, Maggie," Luke said. "You are losing blood and need to be airlifted to a hospital."

Maggie laughed and said, "Like hell. I have lost a little blood, but I am OK. Thank you, Luke."

Luke was in disbelief as Maggie picked up a paddle and began to head her kayak back to the dock.

"You are one tough woman, I mean one tough person," Luke said, politically correcting himself.

Maggie responded with a look of approval.

When they returned to where they had embarked on the tour, the sun was setting, and the office for cabin rentals and the general store were closed. Maggie's legs were rife with black and blue marks, and her ankles and feet were swollen.

"I know you are the female version of Rambo, but Maggie, you need to get off your feet and apply ice to the swollen areas of your legs," Luke said.

Maggie did not argue. She knew Luke was right.

Luke helped Maggie walk to his cabin and placed her on the bed where he propped up her feet and wrapped a couple of clumps of ice from his Yeti cooler in a towel that was placed over her wounds.

Maggie was not accustomed to relying on others for help, but she appreciated the tender loving care that Luke was providing.

Luke asked her if she were hungry.

"I am ravenous," Maggie said. "That makes two of us," Luke said.

He added, "Maggie, I need you to be a good patient. Stay reposed and don't put any weight on your legs. I am going to make a run to the nearest grocery store to buy a couple of steaks for dinner."

Maggie nodded in approval, giving Luke directions to the closest grocery store.

An hour later, Luke returned with a couple of grade A sirloin steaks and two bottles of wine.

Maggie looked at the groceries and said in her southern twang, "You did well, Luke. Just what the doctor ordered."

Luke responded, "I thought you were the patient."

They both laughed at the silliness of their conversation.

Luke grilled the steaks, corn, and baked potatoes on an outdoor grill near the cabin while drinking a bottle of Gallo wine.

As his mind drifted to his boyhood years camping with his father and brothers, Maggie interrupted his nostalgic thoughts. "Luke, there is no way I am going to stay inside this cabin. I am claustrophobic and need fresh air."

Luke carried Maggie to a picnic table within a few feet of the grill. Luke served her dinner and wine, waiting for her to offer compliments to the chef.

"Luke, this is my kind of meal," Maggie said. "Home cooking on an outdoor grill with great company," she said, making brief eye contact with Luke as she sipped wine.

Maggie and Luke were relaxed after a long day in the hot sun and ingesting a couple of bottles of Gallo.

The combination of the wine and ice on her legs had dulled the pain in her lower extremities. She was feeling perky when she handed her glass to Luke and asked for more wine.

He obliged, and then she asked, "So, Luke, tell me how in tarnation you ended up here asking for a tour of the Everglades."

He sheepishly responded there is not much to tell.

"Don't misunderstand me, Luke," Maggie said. "If it were not for you, I would not be alive. Thank God, you were the one on the tour when the gator attacked me."

"OK," Luke said. "I can give you the Reader's Digest version."

Maggie laughed. "The Reader's Digest version. I want to hear the whole story, and the more dirt, the better," she said with a twinkle in her eyes.

Luke told her how a series of unexpected events in his life led him to question his work at PENA, which was the impetus for his separation with Bethany. He explained how his conscience moved him to undergo a conversion from a proponent of big oil to an environmentalist.

Maggie was mesmerized as she listened to Luke. Her intuitive senses told her Luke's story came from the heart.

"You are a good man, Luke," she said. "Be strong and stay the course."

Maggie reached across the table, and Luke clutched her hand. They held hands for several moments as they looked at one another.

Neither Luke nor Maggie made the next move. They respected one another, and a platonic friendship was mutually acceptable for him and her.

But what Maggie shared next with Luke would change his life. She said an environmental group entitled Protecting Florida's Future has been searching for a seasoned lobbyist who truly believes in the cause.

"I think we have found that person," Maggie said. "I know we have."

Maggie explained the job, and Luke was interested.

As they returned to their respective cabins for the evening, Maggie told Luke she would be contacting her PFF colleagues in the morning.

True to her word, Maggie dialed the cell phone number of Cody Lumpkin, chairman of the board of PFF.

Cody recognized Maggie's phone number on his phone and answered, "Hello, Maggie." Before he could get out the next word, Maggie said, "Please tell me you have not hired a lobbyist to head PFF's advocacy efforts."

Cody answered, "I have a few candidates on the radar, but no formal offers yet."

Maggie told Cody about Luke. Cody was intrigued with Luke's conversion from big oil but was unconvinced, even with Maggie's strong endorsement.

Cody asked Maggie to find out if Luke would be available to meet him on his sailboat in Key West tomorrow afternoon.

Cody added, "I am interviewing Mr. McAlarney because your instincts about people are usually spot-on."

Maggie thanked Cody and then told Luke the good news.

"You are on," she said. "Don't blow this."

CHAPTER
15

FOR BETTER OR WORSE

As Luke drove south on Over Seas Highway—the 120-mile stretch of scenic roadway from Homestead to Key West—he admired the view of the Atlantic on the left and Gulf on the right. He was in a state of solace that comes with living life within the framework of his conscience.

Luke smiled at the thought that he no longer was associated with the pestilential mercenaries who are bent on making a buck to the detriment of others.

But he was concerned whether Cody would hire someone from big oil and, secondly, whether the salary would be sufficient for him, Bethany, and the kids.

Luke was not ready to give up on his marriage. He told himself most couples would be separated if they had undergone what he and Bethany had endured.

As Luke approached the Seven Mile Bridge just south of Marathon, he pulled the car off the highway near a landing for campers and boaters. He looked at his phone, and his intuitive senses told him to undertake the initial step to call his estranged wife.

Luke called Bethany, who answered with anxiousness in her voice. "The kids and I have been worried sick about you, Luke. We have not heard from you for days."

Luke, trying to play the sympathy card, responded, "I did not think you wanted to hear from me."

Bethany expressed concern for her husband, but she wanted to know if Luke would be employed in the near future and when she could expect a deposit in their joint checking account.

Luke thought to himself, It is always about the damn money.

But he also realized she was trying to maintain normalcy as much as possible for Bree and Corey, which would require an infusion of money into their bank account.

"I've got some good news," Luke said. "I am waiting," Bethany said with bated breath.

Luke told her he was heading to Key West for a job interview.

Unimpressed, she asked what type of job is headquartered in Key West.

"Charter boat captain and bartender," he quipped.

Bethany always had appreciated Luke's sense of humor and well-timed levity. Amused with Luke's quip, she could not contain her laughter as it audibly ascended into a high-pitched cackle. Once she regained her composure, she said, "At least you have not lost your sense of humor."

Luke laughed too. He could not remember the last time they had laughed together about anything.

"All kidding aside, I am interviewing to be the lobbyist for Protecting Florida's Future, an environmental group," Luke said.

Bethany was silent for a few moments and told Luke she pawned her wedding ring to pay for Bree's initial therapy sessions and their $6,000 monthly mortgage payment, which was due immediately.

"I don't know what to say, Bethany," Luke said. "You did what you had to do. It is my fault for putting you in this financial predicament."

Bethany said this is not about who is reprehensible.

"I told you about the ring because our financial situation is on the brink of disaster," Bethany said.

Luke tried to reassure Bethany he would join the ranks of the employed in the immediate future.

Bethany asked Luke to call her as soon as he hears from PFF. Luke promised to do so.

Bethany placed her phone on the kitchen counter and opened the door of the refrigerator, which was bare except for a carton of eggs and half gallon of milk.

In order to maintain normalcy, Bethany wanted to stock the refrigerator for three squares a day and snacks for the kids to help themselves when they are hungry.

Bethany headed to Fresh for You, a nearby organic grocery store. She piled her cart with an assortment of staples, fruits, vegetables, and other healthy edibles.

Purchasing the groceries was reminiscent of her daily schedule before Luke lost his job and Bree's trip to Jamaica. She needed to have a semblance of consistency in her life, and shopping at the grocery store gave her that.

But as she watched the checkout clerk tabulate the total purchase of more than $400, Bethany suddenly feared whether there were sufficient funds in her bank account to cover the bill.

Almost robotically, she handed the clerk her ATM debit card. Within moments, her fear had come true when the clerk informed her the card had been declined.

Bethany asked why, and the clerk responded, in a voice that carried to other customers waiting in line, "Insufficient funds."

Bethany was embarrassed but became mortified when one of the customers asked, "Bethany, is everything OK?"

Bethany instantly recognized the customer as Gladys Crable, who lived on the same block as the McAlarneys and whose children also attended Montgomery Prep.

Bethany tried to save face by attributing the "insufficient funds" as a technological glitch. The clerk, with polite assertiveness, told Bethany her groceries would be bagged and placed in customer service until she can pay for them.

"That won't be necessary," Gladys said, handing the clerk her debit card. "Place Mrs. McAlarney's bill on my card."

The clerk obliged. Bethany did not know what was worse: to not pay for the groceries or have to be ingratiatingly polite to Gladys, known as a gossip and busybody of Palm Beach's Bel Aire community.

But Bethany swallowed her pride and profusely thanked Gladys.

As the two women were exiting the grocery store, Gladys knew there was a story associated with Bethany's ATM card and suggested they catch up over a latte at a Cuban coffee shop a few blocks away.

Bethany felt compelled to share some general information about Luke's unemployment and their separation.

Gladys listened intently and appeared to be genuinely empathetic. She had the uncanny knack for eliciting information. Before long, Bethany was baring her soul to Gladys, sharing information she never intended to disclose.

Gladys asked, "Why would Luke resign from his job and then leave you and the kids?"

Bethany answered that Luke ambivalently and angrily left at her behest.

"What do you mean by angrily leaving?" Gladys asked, almost as if she were a sleuth on the brink of a clue that breaks the case wide open.

"When I told Luke he needed to move out, he balled his fist up and approached me," Bethany said. "For a few moments, I cowered in fear that he would hit me."

Gladys asked Bethany if she had petitioned the court for a restraining order.

Bethany said she had not. Gladys explained Luke could be precluded from returning home and forced to provide familial financial assistance when reemployed.

"The best of both worlds," Gladys proclaimed.

But Bethany said Luke never hit her.

"The great thing about a protective order," Gladys said, "is the standard to grant it is predicated on the victim's perception of fear, not actual abuse."

Bethany asked Gladys if she had been divorced.

"I have been divorced twice, but three is a charm," Gladys said, flashing her six-carat wedding ring.

Bethany assumed Gladys learned about protective orders during her earlier marriages.

Nothing like a woman scorned, Bethany thought but realized restraining orders are a legal tool to save lives and prevent abuse.

She remembered reading an article that a woman is a victim of a domestic violence every thirty seconds within the United States.

Bethany stared at her latte and then looked at Gladys.

"I do not fear Luke," Bethany said. "For me, it is not about punishing him for something he never did."

Bethany thanked Gladys for the conversation, the latte, and promised to reimburse her for the groceries as soon as possible.

Bethany knew the sale of her wedding ring was only a stopgap to cover immediate expenses. She needed cash, and that meant liquidating assets.

She headed to the Bahia Mar Yacht Club, where she and Luke dry-docked their thirty-one-foot Intrepid cruiser. She met with Hal Johnson, head of sales.

"For the right price, we can sell this boat," Hal said. "There is always a market within the 1 percent club for this type of boat because it is ideal for the Gulf Stream crossings to the Bahamas."

Bethany explained she needed to unload the boat for a profit.

"This could be a problem, depending on what you owe on the boat," Hal said.

He reached in his desk and grabbed a pocket calculator. After working with a few numbers, Hal said she would clear $10,000, including his sales commission.

"You could ratchet up your asking price, but the boat likely would stay in dry dock as you pay for storage, insurance, and maintenance," Hal said. "It is your call."

"OK," Bethany said. "List the boat to sell immediately and please let me know when we have any interested buyers."

She left the yacht club, contemplating her next move for cash. She drove her 2013 Audi A7 sedan to a used car dealership. As she entered the parking lot, two salesmen approached the car.

"Hello, ma'am," Rick Fertig said. "Are you looking for a trade-in?"

Before Bethany could answer, the second salesperson, Billy Bulger, introduced himself. But Rick positioned himself between Bethany and Billy and stated, "The early bird catches the worm." Rick then gestured for Billy to return to the sales office. Billy did so after scoffing and kicking the sand-laden gravel in frustration.

Rick turned his attention to Bethany, who coyly said she might be interested in a trade if the price were right.

"What did you have in mind for your used car?" Rick asked.

Bethany surveyed the parking lot and observed. "Have you ever taken a one-year-old Audi on a trade-in?" she asked.

Rick hesitated and then said, "We take all types of vehicles, domestic, foreign, sedans, SUVs, trucks. You name it, and we have traded for it."

Bethany cut to the bottom line, asking Rick for the trade-in value of the Audi if she purchased one of the cars discounted as specials of the week.

"I'll tell you what," Rick said. "I'll take that Audi off your hands, put you in that Ford Focus, and call it even."

Bethany replied, "You've got to be kidding me."

She walked briskly back to her car, and as she opened the door, Rick yelled, "Wait a minute, little lady. I think we can do business."

Rick then became serious, offering acceptable negotiating terms for Bethany in which she traded in the Audi for a Focus and cleared several grand.

She audibly exhaled and mumbled to herself, "Thank God for some immediate cash."

Bethany was struck with the irony that she would not have been caught dead driving an economy car a few weeks ago. Now she is thankful for immediate cash and a car that could never be mistaken for an Audi.

Bethany giggled like a schoolgirl as she contemplated Luke's reaction when he finds out she traded a European luxury sedan for a used economy car.

On a whim, she sent a text picture of her new car to Luke with the following message: "If less is better and good things come in small packages, then Ford Focus rules! Easy to park too and way less expensive."

As Luke headed toward Big Pine Key, he heard a beep on his phone signaling a text message and saw Bethany's name on his phone screen.

The message from Bethany piqued his interest as he exited the highway. He read the message and then did a double take as he looked at the picture.

"I'll be damned," Luke said. "Hell must have frozen over for Bethany to be driving a little economy car like that."

If Luke were looking for a silver lining for him and Bethany, he just found it.

"The glass may be half full instead of half empty," Luke mumbled to himself, pondering the state of his marriage.

Luke's phone told him the noon hour was approaching. He was about ten miles from Key West and had plenty of time to kill before his 2:00 p.m. interview.

Luke looked around for a coffee shop and noticed a statue of a dolphin about fifty yards from his car. Curiously, he walked toward the statue, adjacent to an inscription.

It stated the statue is a likeness of Flipper, who starred in the 1960s television series about a dolphin, a park ranger, and his two sons. As a young boy, Luke was captivated by the Flipper reruns. He practically memorized every episode.

But Luke did not know Flipper was a female dolphin named Mitzi, who passed away several years after the series ended and is buried beneath the statue.

The last sentence on the inscription stated that additional information about dolphins can be obtained at a marine research center. There was an arrow pointing to a nearby building.

Luke entered the building and paid an entrance fee to watch dolphins showcase their extraordinary abilities in live performances and on video. Some of the footage captured dolphins giving birth, their communicative code, and how the U.S. Navy is utilizing these highly intelligent mammals.

But what Luke remembered most was that the fate of dolphins would be contingent on preservation of the marine ecosystem.

As Luke approached his car, he knew the opportunity to lobby for PFF was not only a job but also his calling.

Luke motored directly to Key West Marina, where Cody's thirty-eight-foot schooner, Natural Lady, was moored. He arrived a few minutes before the scheduled interview and strolled around the marina, inhaling the salt air and gawking at boats.

Luke has been a boating enthusiast for as long as he could remember. He associated boats with nostalgic memories of his early family life when he, his brothers, and father would enjoy offshore fishing, underwater diving, and water-skiing.

And for Luke, there was something therapeutic about maritime ambiance. Throughout his life, whenever he has been stressed, boating has been the remedy to decompress.

As he lithely walked along the dock, avoiding cleats and nautical lines, he had a confidence that his sea legs had not betrayed him with age.

As Luke watched a crewmember from a charter boat cleaning fish on a cutting board at a nearby dock, he heard his name and turned, where he saw Cody standing on the bow of his sailboat.

Cody was anything but an intimidating figure. His ponytail presented a less than macho presence, and his diminutive body weighed no more than 120 pounds soaking wet.

Once they were aboard, Cody gave Luke a quick tour of the vessel. Teak veneer laced the fore, port, starboard, and aft decks. An enclosed wheelhouse, replete with radar and a GPS chart plotter, was positioned between the midship and stern.

A fresh coat of midnight blue adorned the gunwales of the magnificent-looking vessel.

The shear line of Natural Lady reminded Luke of a classic schooner of yesteryear. Down under, there were beautifully coordinated pastel colors in the salon, galley, and V-berth.

Cody introduced Luke to a couple of liveaboards.

Luke was shocked when he made eye contact with Ansel and Claire. Luke instantly remembered them in Steele City, opposing PENA's public relations campaign.

"Luke, Ansel and Claire stay on my boat when they are not on the frontline advancing PFF's agenda," Cody said.

Cody paused then said, "I will be relying on input from Ansel and Claire before formally offering the lobbyist position to you or another candidate."

Cody did not mince words as he asked Luke why he transitioned from big oil to environmentalism.

But Cody quickly followed up on his original question in an attempt to lighten the mood. "You did not come down here under the guise of an environmentalist to see our operation and report back to PENA?"

Luke smiled and responded, "Damn, you are good. What tipped you off that I am a double agent?"

Cody's body language, with one hand on his hip and the other resting under his chin, suggested he did not appear sold on Luke.

Cody asked, "Can a leopard change its spots, and can a big oil lobbyist become an environmentalist?"

Cody added, "I ask the question in light of the fact that Luke lobbied on behalf of PENA for seventeen years and was the point person for SR 538 to be positioned for favorable passage."

Luke became serious as he replied, "I have undergone a transformation in which I questioned my work and the ramifications of it. Maybe I am a changed man. Or possibly I am the same man attempting to be true to my core."

Cody took a breath and said, "That is deep, Luke."

Cody then gestured for Ansel and Claire to infuse themselves into the conversation.

But before they did, Luke added, "My conversion may provide me with a deeper conviction to environmentalism than someone who has not experienced both sides."

Cody, Ansel, and Claire did not respond to Luke's comment.

Luke wondered if they were offended by the comment or just simply caught off guard.

Claire then asked what assurance is there that Luke will stay the course as an environmental advocate.

Luke replied, "In life, there are no guarantees, but what I can tell you is I have undergone a very real conversion in which I have relinquished a lucrative salary to earn far less money to be on the right side of issues."

Cody interjected, "Luke has done his homework. He understands environmental advocacy is a labor of love."

Luke decided if he is going down, he would do so swinging.

"Claire, your question deserves a complete answer," he said. "One of your best friends and trusted colleagues, Maggie Sinclair, is convinced I am the real deal. If you place your faith in Maggie, I ask you place your faith in me too."

Cody thanked Luke for attending the interview and said he would like to confer with Ansel and Claire.

Luke exited the schooner and walked several feet along the dock. Within moments, he received a phone call from Cody. Luke looked and once again saw Cody waving his arms on the bow of the boat.

As Luke boarded the vessel again, Cody said, "It is unanimous. We would like to offer you our lobbyist's position. What do you say, Luke?"

Luke did not hesitate, accepting the offer. He then added, "I know lobbying for PFF is not about getting rich, but I will need a salary to support my family."

Cody placed his hand on Luke's back and said, "We'll work something out." He then asked Luke when he could begin work.

"I need about twenty minutes to call my wife and share the good news and then I can hit the ground running," Luke said.

Cody laughed and said he liked Luke's enthusiasm.

"We need to pull together our project materials so we can get you up to speed on our messaging," Cody said. "This will take a day or so. In the interim, relax, enjoy the Florida Keys, and we will see you in twenty-four to forty-eight hours."

Luke responded, "Thank you, Cody. I look forward to working with you and the PFF team."

Luke then parted company as he walked to his car and called Bethany.

CHAPTER
16

A NEW BEGINNING

Luke anxiously speed-dialed Bethany. When she answered, he feigned disappointment with awkward silence for several moments.

Then Bethany asked the question, "Bad news or good news?"

Luke answered, "Good news if you want your husband to come out of early retirement. I have been offered the lobbyist position for PFF."

Luke anticipated Bethany's next question by adding, "We will negotiate salary. It will be significantly lower than what I was earning at PENA, but we will make ends meet if we live within our means."

Luke did not intend to instruct or lecture, simply to underscore the point they will be able to sustain with some modifications.

"I know you would land on your feet," Bethany said. Luke corrected her. "We have landed on our feet." Luke enunciated the word "our" to emphasize family unity in the spirit of "one for all and all for one."

Bethany asked Luke if he liked her new car. "That car was made for you," Luke joshed.

"I sort of like it," she said. "It is easy to park and good on fuel. In some respects, the car represents the new me."

Luke replied, "I think I am smitten with the new Bethany."

Bethany, without hesitation, said she has an affinity for the newly employed Luke.

They both laughed, marking the second such occasion in twenty-four hours.

Bethany told Luke the kids are anxious to visit him.

"They miss you more than you know, Luke," Bethany said. "I miss them too," he said softly.

Bethany then asked Luke if he were amenable for out-of-town guests in the immediate days ahead.

"Is this a trick question in which I answer yes and then your parents appear in Key West next weekend?" Luke asked playfully.

"How about a package deal—me, the kids, and my old friends from Moultrie?" she kiddingly asked.

"Bethany," Luke said, "you obviously missed the memo that explains I do not embrace the mantra of 'the more, the merrier.'"

Bethany paused then asked, "Well, Luke, would you settle for me and the kids to visit you in Key West next weekend?"

Before he could answer, she added, "We'll understand if you are too busy with the new job and everything."

"The job is important, but it is a job," Luke said. "You, Corey, and Bree are my life. Let's agree the weekend is our family time."

"You've got a deal," Bethany said. She told Luke he could expect her and the kids by or before noon on Saturday.

Luke then called Maggie to share the good news. Maggie had received the news from Cody but did not want to undercut Luke's effervescence.

"I am just glad you did not blow it," Maggie said, deftly exhibiting her dry sense of humor. "Seriously, I am very happy for you and your family."

Luke expressed gratitude for Maggie for cajoling Cody to interview him.

"I will never forget what you did for me," Luke told Maggie. "I owe you big-time and would do almost anything for you."

Maggie playfully but pointedly asked, "What is it with the 'almost' disclaimer. I thought you would be completely beholding to me."

Luke replied, "I stated 'almost' because touring the Everglades in a kayak is a nonstarter."

Maggie responded without hesitation, "If my memory serves me correctly, I was the one who was attacked, not you."

Luke countered, "I vicariously lived through your attack."

"Oh, poor baby," Maggie sarcastically retorted as they ended their call.

Later that day, Luke was fishing in the brackish water in Big Pine Cove. The aesthetic beauty was picturesque as the sun radiated through the palm trees, illuminating on the pristine-clear blue water. The cove was like an underwater odyssey with a smorgasbord of fish distinguished by their size, shape, and stripes as they swam in living color from the surface to the grassy bottom.

Luke was relaxed; his mind spellbound as he absorbed the ambiance. But the therapeutic moment was broken when he heard his cell phone ring.

"Damn it," Luke said, pulling the phone from his pocket and cursing himself for allowing it to interrupt tranquility.

Luke picked up the call. The voice on the other end was Cody's.

Cody said he knew Luke had absorbed a financial hit when he converted to environmentalism but did not know the extent of his family's burden until talking with Maggie.

Per Maggie's suggestion, Cody said he would like to advance Luke $7,500 for moving costs and some carryover money until Luke is receiving a biweekly paycheck.

"It is not a lot of money, but hopefully, it will help," Cody said. "Stop by my boat anytime, and I will have a check prepared for you."

Luke was grateful because the advance appeared to be motivated by a genuine concern for him and his family.

Cody asked Luke to be prepared to report to the office this coming Thursday.

"I look forward to diving in," Luke said.

Cody responded, "I know you do, but I want you to wade in waist-deep before swimming. If you are as good as Maggie says, we want this to be a long-term relationship."

Cody seemed overly concerned about Luke becoming inundated. Maybe, Luke thought, Cody is overly protective or knows how to delegate and manage personnel.

Luke drove to the marina to pick up the advance check. He had big plans. His first order of business was to pay a security deposit to rent a houseboat at the famous Houseboat Row in Key West.

Luke knew renting a houseboat was not practical—insufficient living space and too much maintenance.

"But I am going to kick practicality to the curb," Luke told himself.

Luke's next item on his agenda was to buy a used runabout for fishing the backcountry and diving at the reefs. Bethany had told Luke there was a pending contractual offer from a prospective buyer to purchase the Intrepid.

Luke could rationalize selling the Intrepid, but he was not going to be boatless.

Luke scoured used boat ads and found a 1992 Boston Whaler 17 Montauk with a Johnson 70 horsepower. The boat was a classic in lines and contour but needed a little tender loving care from oxidation in the hot Key West sun.

The purchase of the boat was among a series of fortuitous steps for Luke in recent days. Luke's good fortune may have appeared as if it were serendipitous, but he knew better.

Luke knew all things were possible from the grace of God. He had rediscovered his faith in God, which led him to Our Lady Star of the Sea Parish in Key West. The church was over one hundred years old and one of the buildings on the state's registry of historical landmarks.

Luke also was attracted to the parish because it featured Our Lady of Lourdes Grotto, which is a statue of Mary with a backdrop of a towering stone wall that serves as the center for collective prayers when the enormity of natural disasters are descending on Key West.

Following a Sunday Mass, Luke walked to the Grotto, where he read the inscribed words: "Key West has not experienced a full brunt of a hurricane since the Grotto was dedicated in 1922."

Luke took a deep breath and reflected, "Never underestimate the power of prayer."

He then knelt at the foot of the Grotto and prayed that he, Bethany, and the children would come together in a family-centered manner.

In Luke's newfound pecking order, sandwiched between God and career, was family. There was a void and, with it, a lot of unanswered questions.

Will Bethany and Luke remain separated, and if so, will the kids visit him on weekends? Will Bethany and the kids continue to live in Palm Beach? Or will Bethany and the kids join Luke in Key West?

Luke had no clue as to which scenario would become reality, but he knew Saturday's visit would be a critical step.

Starting a new job, coupled with the impending visit from Bethany and the kids, Luke knew he had to get up to speed with PFF's projects.

He reached out to Maggie for an overview of PFF's priority issues. Maggie told Luke she could speak in terms of big picture in presenting how the mission of PFF applies to pending environmental issues.

She was quick to add that detail was not her forte.

"You know, Luke, the devil is always in the detail," Maggie said as if she were telling Luke something he did not know.

Luke listened politely, even though he knew from countless firsthand experiences that concept builds consensus, and detail is the impetus for division.

Then Maggie reminded Luke that PFF's mission, first and foremost, is to preserve Florida's environment.

"Our media campaign was created to educate the masses about environmentally friendly practices via public service announcements, guest columns in newspapers, specialty publications, social media, speaking tours and through ancillary activities," Maggie said.

Secondly, Maggie said PFF's advocacy has been directed at the local, state, and federal levels.

Anticipating a prospective question from Luke, Maggie said most of PFF's advocacy is before the Florida Legislature, but federal laws can benefit or hinder fragile ecosystems.

"And with federal laws comes federal funding," she said. "Suffice to say, we must have a voice on Capitol Hill."

In addition, Maggie said PFF occasionally supports sister organizations by filing amicus curiae, "friend of the court," briefs.

"We also place our people such as Ansel and Claire on the ground for mobilization efforts to assist in media and PR campaigns," Maggie added.

Maggie appeared amused. Luke asked her what she was thinking.

"Luke, I am not a big fan of Uncle Sam," she said. "Mentioning the feds reminds me of President Ronald Reagan's famous caveat—'the scariest words to hear: I am from the government and I'm here to help.'"

Maggie and Luke both chuckled about the quote.

"Well, President Reagan's quote was certainly prophetic in so far as the federal government attempting to save the Everglades," Maggie said.

She said presidents and members of their cabinets descended upon the Everglades for decades, expressing their heartfelt concern to preserve this natural habitat from industrial toxins, farmland fertilizers, and pollutants from city runoff.

She said federal officials talked a big game and appeared to be concerned how mercury and phosphorous, in particular, would impact the Florida panther and other endangered species as well as the residual effects when contaminated water from the Everglades flows into Florida Bay, thereby jeopardizing the nursing grounds of spiny lobsters.

"But they were like the fox guarding the henhouse," Maggie said.

Maggie, shaking her head in disgust, said, "What the federal government giveth—Everglades Restoration Act—it taketh away by purchasing oil drilling and natural gas rights in select areas of the Everglades."

Maggie looked as if she were staring through Luke when she said, "PFF and other environmental groups are the last vestige between the federal government and big oil to have their way in the Everglades."

Maggie said she recommended Luke for PFF's lobbying position because he understands the inner workings of PENA and can beat big oil and the federal government at their own game.

Luke thanked Maggie for her kind words but added PFF would need to tap into some serious money to combat the likes of PENA and the federal government operatives.

Maggie responded, "You let me and Cody worry about that. We don't have to match them dollar for dollar because the truth is on our side.

"We are on the right side of this issue," she said. "If we stay the course and allow the truth to be told, people will understand that polluting and engaging in gas and oil exploration in the Everglades creates a domino death effect on the food chain as well as deteriorating coral reefs and the fishery in the Keys."

In the end, Maggie said with a deep sigh, "We have to portray the oil and gas zealots for whom they are—profiteers who are willing to wreck havoc on the Everglades and the region's ecosystem for a short-term cash benefit."

Luke did not share Maggie's eternal optimism, but he knew they were on the right side of history.

Luke responded, "This may be one of those issues the longer we can hold big oil and gas at bay, the likelier we will ultimately prevail."

Maggie replied emphatically, "I like the way you think, Luke."

Although fighting for the preservation of the Everglades may be an ongoing crusade for the balance of their lives, there were other important projects they would have to juggle in the immediate future.

Maggie said cruise ship lines are attempting to anchor their passenger liners near Bimini, Bahamas. She added there is no shipping port in Bimini, forcing the passenger liners to anchor off the Bimini coast, thereby jeopardizing the coral reefs and the fisheries.

"Once the reefs are destroyed, they would not be revived for hundreds of years, and that is assuming they are not jeopardized as they undergo restoration," Maggie said.

She added that the Bahamian government is looking at this as a short-term economic benefit rather than long-term environmental degradation.

"In this regard, the Bahamian government, like the U.S. government and virtually every other nation on the planet, is willing to allow for the evisceration of natural beauty under the sea and upset the balance of the food chain for the almighty dollar," Maggie said. "Throw some money their way, and they react like the Whore of Babylon."

Luke laughed in response to Maggie's candor.

"So, Maggie, tell me how you really feel about governments all too willing to sell out the environment for short-term cash," Luke joshed.

Maggie acknowledged her passion but did not apologize for it.

"The day I lose my passion is the day I cease to do this work," she asserted.

Luke told Maggie she is destined to be a lifelong environmental advocate.

"It is in your blood," Luke said. "It is the quintessential you."

She said PFF is collaborating with research groups who have grant-writing resources to infuse five cents on every dollar into Bimini's economy from studies about sharks, dolphins, killer whales, and Atlantis, known as Bimini Wall for its monolithic underwater highway that might be remnants of an earlier civilization.

"We are trying to negotiate with government officials on their terms," Maggie said. "If money is the bargaining chip, then we will try to persuade them that the grant process gives them the best of both worlds—money into the Bahamian economy while protecting the coral reefs and the fishery."

Luke nodded in approval, voicing affirmation for PFF tendering an offer that the Bahamian government can't refuse.

But Luke asked why PFF is involved in a project outside the continental United States.

Maggie said Bimini's proximity to the United States served as a compelling reason for PFF to intervene. She added that there was a sense if the cruise ship lines prevail in Bimini, they will establish a precedent to anchor on coral reefs throughout the Bahamas and Caribbean where there are no ports.

Maggie said PFF's other notable project involves cruise ships in the Tampa Bay Area. She said the flagship of the Scandinavian Cruise Line is a nine-hundred-foot vessel that is expected to make its home port in Tampa.

Maggie explained, the ship—the North American Star—draws too much water to navigate in Tampa Bay and is too tall to make way under the Sunshine Skyway Bridge, which is the gateway into the Port of Tampa. The Scandinavian Cruise Line's solution is to avoid Tampa Bay and the Skyway Bridge by anchoring the North American Star and other large cruise ships along coastal beaches near Fort De Soto Beach and Egmont Key.

Maggie said Fort De Soto is renowned as one of America's most beautiful beaches in the world. And she said the Sun Coast area is paradise for island- hopping to Egmont Key, Anna Maria Island, and Shell Key as well as a natural playground for world-class fishing, diving, and water sports.

"Anchoring ships inland would require massive dredging for the depths to be sufficient for the passenger liners to operate and anchor without running aground," Maggie said. "The dredging would absolutely convolute the aesthetically pleasing turquoise-tinted waters into a sand-laden dull gray with little or no visibility and obliterate the habitat for fisheries near shore."

She cited PFF's environmental impact study that the ramifications of dredging would endure for hundreds of years.

"Make no mistake, the cruise lines are showing themselves to be every bit as callous and mercenary as big oil," she said.

Luke asked her if there is a plan for immediate action.

A couple of articles have been placed in major state dailies within the Sun Coast.

"They are creating a stir," she said. "People are truly aghast that the cruise lines have the audacity, insensitivity, and total disregard for the environment to do this."

Maggie added, "Our short-term strategy is to awaken a sleeping giant by promulgating to every Tampa Bay resident what is at stake. And concurrent to this is for you, Luke, to bring this to the attention of the Florida Legislature."

Luke responded, "Consider it done."

"That's the spirit, Luke," she said. "Maybe we have awakened the sleeping giant in you."

CHAPTER 17

SUNSET CRUISE

Luke was at Cody's schooner at 8:00 a.m. sharp on Thursday for his first official day with PFF.

Luke looked forward to getting to know Cody. Maggie had told Luke that Cody is fair, but highly regarded for his cerebral and fastidious approach, leaving no tangential stone unturned.

Most of Cody's focus related to the Everglades Project and to clarify federal law that protected the Everglades and federal provisions that allowed the government to drill for oil and natural gas on the very land it ostensibly preserves.

Cody asked Luke to determine where federal and Florida land rights conflict with one another and identify federal funding under environmental appropriations codified in statute.

"We might be able to use governmental funding to combat the government's interests to drill in the Everglades," Cody said. "I know it is paradoxical, but then again, the federal government is an exercise in sophistry."

Luke saw a document that was particularly interesting. It stated, among other things, that oil drilling in the Everglades may contaminate aquifers providing water to millions of South Florida residents.

Luke handed the document to Cody who said, "This is a good find and can be very useful for us. Make a note, Luke, oil drilling 'shall' contaminate aquifers instead of 'may' contaminate."

But Luke said "may" is the word cited in the document.

"I know, Luke, but 'may' is too equivocal and 'shall' will help do more in aiding our cause," Cody said. "As you know, Luke, the nature of the business is to push the envelope. All of us are guilty of hyperbole."

Luke had the good sense to bite his tongue the first day on the job with PFF. But Cody's comments forced Luke to supplant his rose-colored glasses with an objective lens as he peered into the inner sanctum of PFF and environmental advocacy.

Luke realized he was kidding himself if he assumed the environmental camp did not engage in manipulation, exaggeration, and half-truths.

At this stage in his career, Luke was convinced all organizations have their share of skeletons in their closets.

But Luke was convinced that there was a distinct line of demarcation between PENA and PFF.

He knew the former is motivated exclusively by profit; the latter is driven to preserve the environment.

"At the end of the day, I'd rather be protecting the environment than maximizing profits for big oil," Luke told himself.

Luke was still in pensive contemplation when Cody asked him to identify private grants that may assist advocacy efforts for PFF.

As Luke was zoned into his private thoughts, which he did occasionally, prompting friends to affectionately dub him Space Cadet, Cody snapped his fingers to garner Luke's attention.

Luke was on a steep learning curve, but for the first time in years, he had an infectious desire to learn. In his heart of hearts, Luke knew he had become ossified in his job with PENA, relying on raw emotion to robotically go through the same routine day in and day out.

Luke was perusing background materials and reading state and federal statutes well into the evening when Cody insisted they call it a day.

But before they did, Cody invited Luke to accompany him to a meeting with South Florida scientists who had sampled mercury and other pollutants from waters in proximity of the Everglades to determine whether the contaminants could be traced to fertilizers from area golf courses.

Luke momentarily paused, wondering if the golf related issue had not been on Maggie's radar.

Luke welcomed the invitation and asked Cody if the runoff from golf courses were a recent development.

"Actually," Cody said, "golf courses have been a long-term culprit. But the movers and shakers behind the development of golf courses promulgate an environmentally sensitive message while monitoring their golf courses in an environmentally insensitive manner."

"We believe the fertilizers from golf courses are debasing waterways and the fisheries," Cody said. "What we don't know is to what extent the Everglades has been impacted. That is why we need to meet with the scientists."

Luke asked if PFF has lobbied the Florida Legislature to impose restrictions to limit fertilizer runoff from golf courses.

"Not yet," Cody said. "That is why we hired you."

Luke responded, "I'll be ready when you give me the green light, Cody."

Luke looked at his wristwatch, which read half past seven.

As Luke packed his materials and stepped onto the dock, he turned to Cody and said, "Think I'll head to the houseboat and jump in the skiff for a sunset cruise. Cody, care to join me?"

Cody thanked Luke for the offer but said sunset cruises tend to make for a late night.

"It has been a long day, and I should hit the sack," Cody wearily said.

Luke drove to the houseboat, which was adjacent to the skiff. As Luke prepared to cast off for a sunset cruise, a weak battery barely turned over the two-stroke outboard.

And as Luke discovered the fuel tank was virtually empty, he knew a sunset cruise this evening was not meant to be.

At first, Luke was disappointed. His favorite time to be on the water was dawn and dusk. But as he cogitated on the situation, he smiled, realizing nixing the cruise on this evening would allow him to proactively top off the fuel tank and have the battery charged so the boat is in turnkey mode for a sunset cruise when Bethany and the kids arrive on Saturday.

The next morning, Luke and Cody continued their discussions from the previous day.

Luke had a good vibe about Cody, who did not manifest Maggie's passion but had a relaxed, confident air about him. He was raised in an affluent Beverly Hills family and inherited a small fortune. A surmountable amount of the money was utilized to initiate PFF and purchase the schooner.

The old Luke would have questioned Cody's decision to spend much of his fortune for the common good. However, the new Luke respected Cody to parlay his money for the greater good of God's creation.

Luke also liked Cody's unpretentious approach.

Cody was the antithesis of autocratic-driven bosses that Luke had known on Capitol Hill. It was refreshing for Luke to work for a self-effacing boss.

Luke was at ease with Cody and, during lunch, shared that tomorrow will be a day of reckoning for him and Bethany.

"Either we will reconcile and become a unified family again or remain separated," Luke said, trying to be emotionally detached from the latter scenario.

After reviewing federal and state statutes, funding streams for grants, and possible marketing strategies well into the evening on consecutive days, both men were ready to knock off work.

As Luke exited from the schooner, Cody called out to him, "Good luck tomorrow."

Luke waved to Cody and headed to Duval Street to purchase Key West ball caps, T-shirts, and shorts for Bethany and the kids.

Luke hoped the gear would serve as an allure for Bethany and the kids to embrace Key West's seductiveness.

Luke then stopped at the grocery store where he purchased ground beef and condiments for tomorrow's cookout.

Luke's alarm awakened him at 6:15 a.m. on Saturday. He was nervous and unsettled about Bethany and the kids visiting. He busied himself by cleaning the outdoor grill, which was located on the stern deck of the houseboat.

Luke anxiously waited for Bethany and the kids to arrive at noon. However, at half past noon, there still was no sign of them.

A few minutes later, Bethany called Luke on his cell phone.

Bethany's voice sounded as if she were exasperated.

"Luke, we have been driving in circles looking for your residence," she hastily said.

Luke neither told her that he lived on a houseboat nor did he share his address was one and the same for all liveaboards at the marina.

He knew telling her such things via a phone call would not bode well.

Bethany asked Luke for his address, and he simply replied, "Sunset Marina Drive."

"That is a strange address," Bethany said. "Are there any street numbers?"

Luke recommended she program "Sunset Marina Drive" into her phone's navigational app and proceed accordingly.

"I will keep a sharp eye out for you and the kids," Luke told Bethany.

In a few minutes, Luke saw a white Ford Focus enter the marina parking lot.

Bethany drove through the parking lot, looking for a home.

But there were only vessels moored at docks.

"This can't be the right location," Bethany told Corey and Bree.

Corey replied, "Maybe Dad is living on a boat."

Bethany gave Corey a look of utter intolerance for his aforementioned comment.

"Don't even think that," she sternly said. "Hopefully, your father has the good sense to rent a real home with a concrete foundation on land."

As the Focus appeared to make a U-turn to exit the marina parking lot, Luke leaped from the houseboat to the dock and sprinted onto the parking lot, waving his arms and shouting.

Bethany, Bree, and Corey heard "stop, stop" and collectively looked to see a man running toward them.

"Is that Dad or some crazy man running around yelling with his hands in the air?" Bree asked.

Bethany, who appeared amused, said, "I am pretty sure that is your dad."

As Bethany and the kids exited the car, Luke hugged each of them.

Then stepping back, he said, "Welcome to my humble abode," as he gestured toward the houseboat.

"I believe the operative word is 'humble,'" Bethany said with no hint of levity in her voice.

Once aboard the houseboat, Luke served Bethany a glass of grocery store Gallo wine and provided the kids with iced tea.

They sat on the stern deck, relaxing on a lazy Saturday afternoon and admiring the view. Then Bethany became serious, turning to Luke and taking a breath.

"Bree desperately would like to transition from Palm Beach following the fiasco in Jamaica," she said. "Corey is like you, loves the sea. Key West would be a natural fit for him."

Luke then asked, "How about you, Bethany?"

Bethany momentarily looked away, then made eye contact with Luke.

"I have done a lot of soul-searching these past several weeks," she said. "I realize I miss you and want our family to be whole."

Luke embraced Bethany, and he motioned for the kids to join in a group hug.

But Bethany added in a no-nonsense voice, "Let's get one thing straight."

Bree and Corey looked at one another nervously, not knowing whether their mother's ensuing words would divisively impede the Kumbaya moments in the here and now and, moreover, divide and conquer any notion of a unified family in the foreseeable future.

As all eyes fixated on Bethany, she said, "We are not going to live on a houseboat, which is nothing more than a floating double-wide trailer."

Bethany, attempting to repress a smile, added, "The McAlarneys will not be a white trash family."

Bethany said she is willing to cede her appetite for affluence for a more palatable and reasonable lifestyle.

"I no longer have to have the big home and all that goes with it," Bethany deftly said. "I've been there, done that."

She hesitated, then with a twinkle in her eyes, said, "It is not the size of the house that matters most, but the love in it."

At that moment, Luke realized as he was attempting to be true to his conscience, Bethany was undergoing a transformation too. Power, privilege, and riches were giving way to a more modest and simpler way of life.

Luke looked at his wife, who could no longer contain her smile and approached him, wrapping her arms around his neck and clarifying her request. "What I am asking for is a home on solid land with a couple of bedrooms, a kitchen, and family room."

Luke paused then replied, "I am all in to purchase a house that we can afford and does not break the bank."

Luke kissed Bethany and asked, "Do you know what this means?"

Bethany feigned coyness and said, "Why no, Luke, what does this mean?"

"It means, my dear, you are stuck with me," he said.

She replied, "I would have it no other way."

The McAlarneys cooked hamburgers on the houseboat and then casted for baitfish until the early evening.

As Luke looked at the sun, he estimated there was about an hour of daylight.

Luke asked Corey to untie the dock lines from the skiff as he cranked over the outboard.

"All aboard," Luke called out as he waited for Bethany and the kids to be seated on the hardwood bench seats before shifting the engine in gear, meandering the boat through a no-wake zone.

Corey asked if the skiff is too old and too small for the rough waters beyond the coral reefs.

"She's a little worn but should have no problem handling the two-to-three-foot chop in and around the reefs," Luke said.

Luke added that a seventeen-foot skiff is enough boat to cruise to their desired fishing and diving spots.

"That sounds like something Grandpa would have stated," Corey said.

Corey's observation instantly resonated with Luke, whose father, Dermot, was fond of saying: "It is not the size of the boat that matters most, but whether it can get you to where you want to go."

Luke turned to Corey and said, "Your grandfather is probably smiling from above if he can see us in this little skiff, together and happy."

For a few moments, Luke felt as if there were stillness in the air as he reflected on his father's passing nearly a year ago. Luke was very close to his father, and each day, in which he was confronted with a dilemma, he asked himself, "What would Dad say if he were here?"

Luke felt rueful as he reflected, When our parents pass away, a part of us dies with them.

As they passed from the no-wake zone to open water, Luke throttled the boat on plane and contemplated the words he intends to live each and every day for the rest of his life.

The words, from notable author Leo Babauta, remind Luke to stay true to his well-formed conscience: "The life you have is a gift. Cherish it. Enjoy it to the fullest. Do what matters most."

Luke was more content and at peace than ever. He smiled, looked upward to the heavens, and whispered inconspicuously, "Thank you, God, for countless blessings."

www.ingramcontent.com/pod-product-compliance
Lightning Source LLC
LaVergne TN
LVHW041947070526
838199LV00051BA/2941